A Daughter Of Israel
By
Frederick Merrick White

I

All through the beauteous summer, with its sunshine and ruddy glow of warmth, there had been misery and despairing want among the countless toilers, the thousands of human bees in the smoky hive called Westport; but in the country there was peace and restfulness, a smell of innumerable flowers in the fields fragrant with blossoming, for the hay harvest had been gathered and the grain was shot with gold in the sloping cornlands above the ruby sea. In Westport the same silence lay; but it was the cascade of starvation, for the men were 'out,' and all the clang of countless hammers and whirr of machinery was still. At the street corners there stood sullen, moody crowds staring hunger in the face, and murmuring below their breath as the soldiery, with long step and jingling spurs, went by. The steam cranes no longer slid their heavy burdens into the deep holds of ships, for the docks were quiet as the streets, while in the tidal canal, with waters now pure as crystal, vessels lay waiting for the sea, with their tapering masts faint as gray needles in the ambient air. Now there was no hurry and bustle there, but only three children waving their feet in the lapping waters.

There were other children in the distance playing, yet with no zest in their recreations; but these three seemed to be apart from the others, for they were better clad and had no hollowness of eye or pinched natures as the others.

There were two boys and a girl, the eldest boy perhaps sixteen, the others apparently his juniors by the brief span of two years. They did not look like English lads, for their faces were bolder cut and their eyes darker—the aquiline group of countenance which denotes the chosen people. The senior of the little group would have been handsome had it not been for a certain greedy, crafty look on his thin colourless lips, and the deformity between the shoulders. Abishai Abraham, conscious of his ugliness, conscious also of his crooked mind, cared but little for that, and took a pride in his own misfortune from his earliest years—for child he had never been—his hand had been against all men's, and as against his. For the body has a tendency to warp the mind.

The other two—Hazael and Miriam—had the flashing eyes and inherent boldness of their ancestors; but no such curse spoilt the suppleness of their perfect limbs. In their mild gipsy beauty they would have made a study for an artist as they sat there bathing their feet; Hazael, with head thrown back, and long black hair sweeping from his forehead. But the girl sat upright, swinging her white feet backwards and forwards, with no shield from the fierce sun but her luxuriant ebon locks but looking straight before her with fearless, flashing eyes—a child in years, perhaps, but with a face and figure almost womanly, and from her low forehead to her scarlet mouth giving promise of a coming loveliness, such as Anthony fell down and worshipped, and for love of whom a kingdom fell.

Yet she had no consciousness of this, seated there playing in the crystal brine and looking down into the resplendent liquid; saw no beauty there or future triumph—nothing but the smiling, treacherous water.

"Miriam is admiring herself," said Abishai, parting his lips in a faint sneer.

"Well, what then?" Hazael retorted, eager to defend his twin sister. "You don't expect her to admire you, I hope. Miriam is going to be the most beautiful woman in Westport, and then you can walk out together for people to see the contrast."

"And what is beauty, after all?" asked the cripple, usually unmoved, as he stirred the water with his crutch. "You can't live on it; you can't sell it."

Miriam brought down her glowing eyes from the contemplation of a lofty mast pinnacle, where they upshot like a forest in the sky, and regarded the speaker with a look of infinite disdain.

"You would buy and sell everything," she said. "And would imprison the sunshine and barter it over a matter. Why?"

"Because everything is valueless besides money. Where should we have been now, the seed of Abraham, if it had not been for our wealth; if we had not held together and helped one another? What chance would the chosen people have had beside the Gentiles but for their money? Why do they flatter us, and fawn upon us, when their extravagance has left them penniless?"

"And hate us because we take advantage of their misfortunes," Hazael exclaimed. "That is the ban upon our race."

"They are not all so bad," said Miriam, softly. "I sometimes think the blame is not entirely with them. If it had not been for Mr. Lockwood we should not be so happy and contented now."

"And if it had not been for his friend, Sir Percival Decie, we should have no felon's taint hanging over us either. We could have looked the whole world in the face and not been ashamed of our father."

Miriam was silent for a moment; for there was a deeper shade on the clear olive skin, and a flush of pink painted on her cheek, as a blush rose deepens in the sun. Her recollection seemed to have gone back years to the time when she had yet another parent.

"I do not see how we can blame him," she said, with a sense of justice so rare in woman. "Sir Percival was hard, perhaps, yet it seems to me that since father has gone we are happier."

She said this hesitatingly, as one fears to utter praise. Hazael made a great splashing with his feet to show his approbation of this sentiment. But Abishai shut his thin lips the closer, and there came into his eyes a look merciless and vindictive, and strangely out of place for one so young.

"You think so because your memory is not so long or conscious as mine. But I remember, though I was only ten. Father never forgave an injury, and he will not forget this one. You wait and see." And then the speaker sank his voice to the softest whisper. "A time will come when Sir Percival Decie shall regret his cruelty to the last day of his life."

"You were always father's favourite," Hazael observed—"so Mother says."

"He liked me best," Abishai replied, with unconscious pride. "He knew I should grow up like him. He taught me to always save a penny where I could; how to deal and bargain, and how to tell precious stones. And I have profited by his teaching. None of you can show anything like this."

Abishai, after some painful writhings, produced a little leathern bag from the recesses of a secret pocket, and, opening it, laid three stones upon the palm of his dusky hand. They glittered and sparkled in the sun like dew upon the hedgerows, but their shine was no brighter than the shimmer in the owner's eyes. Hazael drew his breath with a sudden gasp of admiration, such as his race always have for diamonds; but Miriam drew no closer than she was impelled by a woman's curiosity.

"Where did you get them?" Hazael faltered, in fascinated wonderment. "They are not your own, surely?"

"They are mine," Abisahi replied. "When will you have anything so precious? Never. Look how they glitter in the sun; there is no falseness or deception there. That is what my father taught me. I bought these from a sailor: ay, so cheap, too. Only two pounds they cost me, but I would have had them if it had been ten times the money. Look at that white stone: how it gleams! I would not take fifty pounds for them now."

"What are you going to do with them?" Hazael asked, still lost in admiration.

"They are the first step to fortune. I shall change them into money, and lend it out in small sums; I shall treble it in a year, and treble that in another year, until——"

Abishai's eyes had commenced to glow as he conjured up this alluring prospect. In imagination he saw himself rich and powerful. This was his darling ambition. Then something splashed in the water, sending a wreath of silver spray over the earnest group; and, looking up, they saw a crowd had gathered round them. By them there stood two girls: one pale and frightened, the other with a cut upon her forehead and a thin purple streak on her face. Miriam turned to them with haughty disdain. The newcomers were of the same consanguinuity, but between them existed a deadly feud, not so tragic, but as lasting and bitter, as the feud of the Capulets and Montagus.

"Ruth and Aurora Meyer," Miriam cried, "how could you come near us?"

"Do you think I wanted to come," cried the wounded one, wiping her stained face. "I came to warn you. Look there!"

The crowd gathered round were mostly children, with the hard marks of hunger in their faces, but cruel and desperate as if they had been a besieging army. They came closer, throwing stones and dirt at those hated Jews; hated the more now that there was so painful a contrast between them. The gaunt hollow eyes and paled faces looked mischief, for they were desperate and cared not for gaol, for that at least meant food. Presently, one bolder than the rest threw a stone, striking Hazael upon the temple.

And the hot blood in his veins fired up at this stinging blow, for the hatred between the rival factions was normal. With a cry he sprang forward, and rushed briskly upon the opposing force.

The fray became general; for there was no pluck wasted on either side. Hazael, with every nerve in his body thrilling, and supported by Abishai, who used his crutch with disastrous effect, fought bravely on. Even the girls sank their enmity in face of this common danger and returned blow for blow.

But the opposing army had too genuine a contempt for the rules of war or difference of sex to disdain force in return, and by very stress of numbers were bearing down the little knot of dark-hued Hebrews. It was, classically speaking, horrid war between hunger and plenty, Jew and Gentile, Demos and Order, and the tribe of Abraham were getting the worst of it.

At this fateful moment, startled by the din of combat from the dim shade where he had been sleeping, a lad appeared and, taking in the situation at a glance, bore down upon the fray. His limbs were lithe, and spoke of power, though upon his pale, clear-cut features there was no trace of sympathy or passion.

With quick resolution he decided to throw his influence into the weaker scale, not from any love of fair play, but rather that instinct which impels most of us to reside with the more respectable cause. Unseen, he approached the group, and with a few dexterous twists slipped through the crowd and stood by Hazael's side.

The effect of this unexpected aid was speedily felt. The stranger wasted little time in unnecessary diplomacy, but singling out the plebeian leader, attacked him with such force and fury that he was fain to lie down and cry for mercy. Abishai marked the weight of their ally's blows, delivered not so much in honest fight, but struck with a nervous weight which delighted the hunchback's vindictive soul.

He whirled the crutch round his head with renewed vigour; gradually the crowd fell back, and then, with a parting jeer and a volley of stones, melted away. For a time the victors regarded their preserver in breathless silence. It was Miriam who came forward at length, holding out her hand as a queen might extend her fingers for a favourite courtier to kiss.

"We thank you," she said. "This is very good of you."

"I have done nothing," the youth replied. "Anything is better than lying down yonder almost asleep and starving."

He was leaning a granite block listlessly, with his left hand hanging inertly by his side. His face they saw was paler than its wont, as if he was undergoing some acute pain, which served to intensify the refinement of his features. His head was held with a certain easy carriage; the eyes were fearless, the lips were thin and cruel, and spoilt an otherwise pleasant countenance.

And yet in his tattered garments he looked almost a gentleman. Abishai propped the crutch under his chin, and regarded the stranger earnestly from under his deep-set eyebrows.

"You fight well," he croaked, with a pleased recollection of the ringleader's discomfiture. "I am strong, but I cannot strike like that."

"I am used to it," the stranger replied, carelessly. "One does get used to it in knocking about the country. I used to travel the fairs with a company of pugilists. I was the infant wonder, you mind. Sometimes I got badly hurt; but I learnt something, too."

He raised his hands in an attitude of self-defence, but dropped them again in a sudden spasm of pain. Miriam, with a woman's quick intuition, saw that he was hurt, and, coming to his side, took his hand in hers.

"You have broken your wrist," she said. "Why did you not say so before?" She turned to the other two girls, who were still standing in the background. "Ruth and Aurora Meyer, how dare you stay here? Go! Boy, what is your name?"

"My name?" he laughed, slowly. "I have no name yet. But you may call me Speedwell—Philip Speedwell, for want of a better."

"Then, Philip Speedwell, you must come with me."

She turned and led the way, beckoning him to follow her. Hazael said nothing, but Abishai crept alongside Miriam with a scowl upon his face.

"Are you going to take him home?" he asked, incredulously.

"Of course. Has he not fought for us, and been injured in our cause? Mother can see to his wound, and give him something to eat. Ah! even then, Abishai, there will be enough for you."

"Abishai would steal the food from a dog," Hazael exclaimed, turning to the stranger, who had listened to this dialogue with a faint smile. "He has no gratitude. No wonder men hate our people."

"We always hate those who are better off than ourselves. I thought you were Jews when I heard your names. So your brother would steal the bone from a dog? Well, at present, so would I. But he should have a little feeling for me, because on my mother's side I, too, am one of you."

II –

Had the haughty families, Montagu and Capulet, been next door neighbours—to use our homely idiom—the disasters of the unhappy lovers would probably have been still more intensified in those good old days when gentlemen carried rapiers and were hypersensitive of their name and honour. But in the broad light of the nineteenth century, the exigencies of Society demand a different method of maintaining a respectable family feud, and the belligerents may live side by side without danger of mortal combat and the slitting of wizends. Certain it is that the Abrahams and Meyers hated one another with the same rancour as their more patrician prototypes, though they dwelt side by side, and pursued the same occupation of general dealers and pawnbrokers. The houses, low-browed and half-timbered, with beetling gables, had originally been one shop, standing in Horton-street, and were, perhaps, the only relics of the Middle Ages at present remaining in Westport. The shops were dark and stuffy, by reason of the kind of trade carried on there, and in the back part of the premises, the portion devoted to pawn broking, there were sundry little boxes where the more timid might retire to bargain with Rebecca Abraham for a loan on any valuable they might be fortunate enough to possess, to say nothing of the advantage of a side door leading into a lane, thus ensuring privacy and protection against the nagging of slanderous tongues. Another lane ran by the side of Meyer's establishment, and their private boxes were situated in exactly the same place, with a few holes bored in the wainscot for ventilation, so that anyone of a curious turn doing business in one place could hear what was being transacted in the other. On the broad, shallow landing, four bedrooms led out on either side, except one, where a partition had been erected when the houses had been made into two; and here was a door, connecting the two establishments, but which now had been carefully barred for years.

Between the long, narrow counters Miriam led the way, followed by the stranger, Hazael coming close behind, and Abishai lingering after him, banging his crutch with an angry jerk upon the floor, and scowling hideously. The guide led the way to a little room behind, where an elderly woman was seated, with a pile of silver lying on the table before her. These she was polishing in a loving, tender fashion with a chamois leather. Her hair was quite white, and there were lines upon her face graven by years of care and trouble. Her eyes were still full and flashing, her nose such as you see only in one race.

"Mother," said Miriam, "I have brought you a friend."

Rebecca Abraham looked up swiftly, then down again, saying nothing in reply. She had a bracelet in her hand, rubbing the tarnished surface with her long, polished fingers. Abishai tapped with his crutch again, and gazed at his mother in fond expectation, waiting for her to speak.

"A friend in the land of the Gentile is like the mirage of the desert, bringing hope only to increase despair. We have no friends: for is not our hand against every man's, and every man's against us!"

She pushed back the white masses of hair from her forehead. There was a foreign accent in the words, as one who speaks a tongue not her own. Then, as if the matter were dismissed, she ran her long lithe fingers round the ornament again, till it shone like a white gleam in the gloom. The stranger stood looking on totally unmoved. It was all one to him whether he was sleeping under the shade of a sail by the quay or resting in one of the carven chairs with their tarnished crimson furniture.

"You are wrong, mother," Miriam spoke again.

Then, without waiting for any reply, she told the story of the battle by the docks. Rebecca listened to the tale, though her hands were never idle. When it was finished, she swept the heap of silver aside, and taking a fair, white cloth, placed it upon the table and set out food.

"You are hungry?" she asked. "Then sit down and eat."

Nothing loth, for hunger conquers all feelings of diffidence, Speedwell took his seat, and turned with a wolfish look to the cold meats before him.

He had eaten nothing since the previous afternoon, but from stern experience he knew the effects of ravenous feeding. So, in a meditative way, he ate slowly and deliberately, and presently his eyes began to wander round the place in easy contemplation. Miriam, without seeming to notice his gratitude, waited upon him, cutting up his meat, for his injured hand lay upon the table helpless. Then, with a contented sigh, he lay back, and, from force of habit and an aptitude for finding comfort in strange places, he fell asleep.

"A good meal," said Abishai, regarding the scraps regretfully; "an enormous meal. Nearly enough to keep us for a day. But Miriam was always wasteful and thoughtless. If it had been me——"

"If it had been you!" Miriam exclaimed, in ineffable disdain: "you would have left him to stave and rot for all you cared. Yes; and he may have saved your life. And our own flesh and blood, too."

In the dim room it was almost too dark to distinguish the slumbering lad's features. Rebecca Abraham drew closer and peered eagerly into his face, like one who has been searching for a thing long and hopes to have found it.

"It was not in the eyes," she said, speaking to herself. "No, I cannot see it. Miriam, my child, how do you know this?"

"He told me he was one of us, mother, though his name is not one of ours. You are not angry that I brought him here?"

"No, I am not angry, my child. We must try to pay our debts, even those of gratitude, though 'tis poorly expressed. The lad is homeless, you say; but we are too poor to have a burden laid upon us."

"You need not fear for that," answered Miriam. "He will not stay here, being one of the wanderers from place to place, living on the bread of charity."

"A thief maybe; perhaps one who knows the inside of a gaol," Abishai observed, his head still propped upon his crutch; "a common, ragged vagabond, who comes here to spy out the house, and rob us in the night."

The shrill voice seemed to rouse the sleeping lad, for he stirred in his chair and opened his eyes. He fixed them upon the hunchback with a glare which caused him to start back affrighted, fearful lest his words had been heard. The outcast smiled bitterly.

"I have been starved and beaten," he said. "I have slept in the open air, when I might have known warmth and comfort; but I am no thief, neither do I know the inside of prison walls. Yes, I heard you; the sleep of one who moves from place to place is light, like that of the curs he herds with. But I am no thief, Abishai Abraham."

"How do I know that?" asked the cripple, glancing suspiciously, yet shrinking back, somewhat abashed. "How can you prove that?"

"When you bought those diamonds last night, in that quiet place down by the docks, how easy it would have been to rob you then. You did not know how close I was to you; it was easily done. You will think better of me when you know me as your father does."

Rebecca dropped the bracelet she was noiselessly polishing, and gazed at the speaker with wild, affrighted eyes.

"You have seen him?" she faltered.

Miriam and Hazael turned to one another almost fearfully. Abishai had folded his hands upon his crutch, his eyes bright and exultant; but in their different emotions they did not heed the strange ague which seemed to have smitten their mother in every limb.

"I have known him some weeks now," the stranger said, lowering his voice to an impressive whisper. "Never mind how. Partly because he was kind to me, I did all I could for you to-day. We parted some time ago."

"This is some strange mistake," Rebecca said, with uneven voice, "because the father of my children is not——"

"At liberty, you would say. Strange you have not heard. Saul Abraham escaped nearly two months ago from Portland."

For some moments there was a painful silence, broken only by the sound of laboured breathing. Rebecca turned away, so that the declining red rays of sunlight falling through the dim panes should not show the white, despairing agony of her face.

"It matters not how we met," Speedwell continued, "but we were useful to one another. Then we parted, little expecting to meet again, till I saw him last night."

"Here in this very place?" Rebecca asked.

"Yes; down by the docks. Abishai there almost touched us as he passed."

"The will of Heaven will be done!" she murmured; "for whom the Lord loveth he chasteneth. I have prayed that after all these years——What is that?"

She pressed her hand to her heart, which was beating wildly. There was a sound of a heavy step in the shop coming towards them. They sat almost afraid to move, till the latch was raised, and the new-comer entered. Fresh from the bright sunshine, he could see nothing but a group of silhouettes, and so their emotion was lost upon him.

The deepening light showed them a man of more than medium height, with a benevolent face, clean-shaven, and fringed with silvery hair. He wore upon his head a broad felt hat, which he had not removed on entering. He had on a long waistcoat reaching almost to his knees, a ruffled shirt-front, and a full skirted coat of sombre brown. His nether man was clad in homespun breeches, finished off with gray knitted hose and heavy shoes latched with steel buckles. As he stood there, with his large white hands folded behind him, he might have posed for the embodiment of prosperity, in which, indeed, his looks would not have belied him, for Mark Lockwood was reputed to be the wealthiest manufacturer in Westport; a generous friend, a good master, albeit an uncompromising Quaker.

By this time Rebecca had recovered herself. She came forward with a gesture of humility almost Oriental, and placed a chair for the new-comer. Then raising the skirt of his coat to her lips, she kissed it reverently, and, folding her hands, waited for him to speak.

"I have come, friend Rebecca, because I hear that some of my people have been molesting thee," said Mr. Lockwood. "They are a wild lot, and take great delight in the maltreating of innocent persons. They have been assaulting thy children. I trust no grievous harm has been wrought."

"No harm, I thank you, master," Rebecca answered. "You know how they hate us always, and how much the more now that my children are well nourished while they are starving."

"The stiff-necked will not hearken to the voice of reason," returned the manufacturer. "Verily, this strife between master and man grieves me sorely. Even my mediations have failed to heal the breech, and yet we must have justice as well as they. But it was an evil day for Westport when the labourer listened to the voice of the charmer. But thou hast not told me, friend, how thy children came off unscathed."

In a few words Rebecca told the simple story. Abishai stood gloomily in the background, but Miriam and Hazael drew their champion forward, where the light might fall upon his face. Mark Lockwood clasped his hands round one knee, and regarded the lad not unkindly for a brief space.

"Thou'rt well-favoured, boy," he said, at length, "and I like the expression of thy face. Tell me thy name, please."

"I am called Speedwell," was the haughty reply. "What is yours?"

"Nay; but I did not mean to wound thy feelings," Mr. Lockwood observed, with a gentle smile, "nor do I seek to pry into thy affairs. But I like spirit in a lad. Art willing to work?"

"I am willing to do anything to get an honest living, sir. The question is, are you willing to give me the chance?"

The merchant rubbed his chin, looking meanwhile into his questioner's face with shrewd, smiling gray eyes. He was too natively independent himself to despise that spirit in others. But the spindles were silent now, the workshops empty. It was no time to seek for work in Westport.

"Thy question is a fair one," he answered, at the same time taking a purse from his pocket, "though it is somewhat difficult to answer. But this unfortunate strife cannot last long, and then I can do something for thee. Art thou willing to tarry here?"

Abishai drew a deep, anxious breath as he awaited the answer to this question. That his mother would do anything Mark Lockwood asked he well knew, but the idea that the stranger might so decide was gall to his miserly soul. Still, the sight of the purse was an evidence of benevolent intention.

"I am willing to stay here," Speedwell answered at length.

"Then that is well. Friend Rebecca, can'st thou find the lad board and lodging till I am in need of his services."

"It is but a small favour you ask," replied the Jewess, fervently. "I have not forgotten. If you desire he may stay, and welcome."

"Nay, I do not mean that thou shalt bear the burden. Here is money sufficient for the lad's present needs, and to purchase him suitable habiliments."

Mark Lockwood laid some gold upon the table. Rebecca, after a mental struggle, put out her hand, gathering up the coins with a low murmur of thanks. She fain would have refused the money, but the instinct of race was too strong within her, and moreover—like Isaac of York's silver—the sovereigns were crisp and clear. The manufacturer, with his hands still clasped behind him, regarded Speedwell kindly, though the benevolence was tempered with some worldly shrewdness. Then, patting his new protege upon the back, he turned and left the room without another word.

"You are fortunate among men," Rebecca said at length. "You have found a master such as few toilers have. Serve him well, and he will serve you well all the days of your life."

"As he treats me so I shall repay him." Speedwell answered, with a quick flush. "He seems to be a good man."

"Ay, that he is," Abishai cried. "Never a better in Westport."

A fire had lighted in the hunchback's eyes like a frosty glitter of winter stars. But there was no ring of sincerity in his voice beyond the warmth fired in him by the sight of the red gold.

III –

Darkness had fallen on the docks. Gradually the tapering masts had melted into the fading sky till the cordage became faint as gossamer, and the dark shining hulls reposed shimmering against the evening mists coming up from the sea on the breast of the tide. The ghostly light faded away; distance was annulled save where a lantern gleamed in nebulous circles.

There was nothing moving except the shadows, or so it seemed, till a black mass crept out from between the sheltering haven of the wood piles and crept cautiously along the granite quay. In the fell gloom it might have passed for a hunted animal; but it was worse than that, being a hunted man. Presently, he moved on again, crouching close, for a splash of light fell upon him from a ship's deck.

It was not a pleasant face which turned towards the golden light. The eyes were black and tempestuously wild, with defiant fear radiating the purple iris. The skin was darker for the wrinkles graven upon it, the nose curving like a bow from the forehead, horribly aslant to the gibing thin lips. His frame was closely knit and, from the hilarious swing of the arms, powerful; for he tossed them from time to time over his head as if the sensation was a new and pleasing one. For a second he scowled at the light, then plunged into the gloom again, pressing upon his way till he reached the water edge, and, casting away his shoes, dangled his bruised feet in the fair water. At the sound of the gurgling wash, an object standing so still that the fugitive had taken it for a capstan, suddenly moved, whistling softly.

"Is it safe to be sitting there in the darkness?"

"Safer than the sun for some of us," the convict replied with a deep respiration of relief. "Is that you, Phil?"

"Yes, more fool me, when I might have been safe in bed."

"But you dared not stay away, my dear; you dare not when old Saul wants you. Have you brought the tobacco and the brandy?"

He chuckled with dry horrid glee, crowing the more as the new comer produced sundry packets from his pockets. Then, filling up his pipe, he cautiously struck a match, and shading it from sight with his horny claw, ignited the tobacco. As he threw the light away, the wisp-like flame lit up for a second the face of Philip Speedwell.

He was pale and ill at ease; all his flinty assurance gone. The convict sucked his pipe, and applied himself with affectionate zest to the flat bottle in his hand, till he became loquacious under its cheering influence.

"Why don't you talk?" he demanded. "Let me hear your sweet voice. Ah, it is all very well for you, who can show your face anywhere! I haven't spoken to a soul since last night. Been lying under the piles all through this accursed daylight, with every footfall bringing my heart up into my mouth; fancying a hand upon my shoulder every minute. What a fool I've been; and only another eighteen months to wait for my release. And now, if I get caught, it'll mean five years. You were wise to wait till your time was up."

The outcast rambled on in his dry, rusty tones, grateful for the blessing which had brought him someone to talk with. It seemed a positive luxury after those awful quiet hours, to feel the presence of a companion.

"Don't talk like that about me," Speedwell returned, moodily.

"Well, I suppose you won't deny you have been in gaol?"

"And how much the better shall I be for owning it? Besides, now I have a chance to turn honest—ay, and mean to."

The convict lay back, his sides heaving, and face working with every sign of unbounded hilarity, though no sound issued from his cavernous throat.

"Ah, that's just the way you used to gammon the chaplain," he said, in a tone of pleased retrospection. "You always were an artful chap, but no use to try and bamboozle me. Besides, we couldn't spare you. But if there is anything in the wind, let's have it."

Saul Abraham listened in unbounded astonishment to Speedwell's tale. For a time he was perfectly silent, his eyes glaring in the dark like a cat's. Partly he was inclined to envy his companion's good fortune, but more especially he speculated upon the possible advantage that might spring from it.

"There is something in the honesty dodge, after all," he ruminated, softly. "Anyway, you had better stay where you are for the present. If anything happens to me"—here he shuddered—"you might be useful here. If old Lockwood has taken a fancy to you, your fortune is as good as made."

"What are you going to do?" asked Speedwell, with anxiety ill-disguised. "You can't hang about here much longer."

"Don't want reminding of that," the convict growled. "Besides, you don't suppose I found my way here because I was dying for a sight of my family? I came for something better—revenge. And you've got to help me. Listen."

It was only the deep bay of a dog, reverberating in widening echoes on the still night air. Abrahams drew a respiration of relief.

"My nerves are not what they used to be," he continued. "If it hadn't been for what I am bound to do, I should have given myself up long ago. I dare say you wonder what it has got to do with you. And that's why I brought you here. To begin with, your name ain't Speedwell at all."

"That I know," answered the lad, moodily. "The question is, what is it?"

"Just what I'm coming to. Now, being relations——"

"Relations?"

"Nephew, don't make that noise, you gaol bird? Do you want the whole town down upon us? Yes, you're my nephew, and I congratulate you upon your uncle. Your mother was my sister, your father was in the Royal Blues, once Captain Decie, brother of Sir Percival Decie, of The Moat, close here. And that's the man you and I have to crush. Time was when I was young and confiding, though you wouldn't think it now; when I was the Captain's valet, and thought him the finest gentleman alive. Why, even now, if he was to come here and say the word, I believe I should get up and follow him like a dog. But I am talking about what happened years ago, and it is getting late. Well, the Captain was a gay young man, different to his brother, Sir Percival, and lived in London, ruffling it with the best of them, spending his money like water, but pleasant and open-handed to his servants. Lord, we would have gone through fire and water for him. It was one time when we were staying at The Moat that the first thing happened. My mother kept the old shop where you have been to-day, and my sister—your mother that is— lived with her. When I fell in love with my wife, and asked the Captain's permission to get married, he laughed in his pleasant way, and said he must come and salute the bride. So down he came to our house, and made himself at home directly, flirting with Rachel—your mother again—but we thought nothing. And when she disappeared, six months later, I never suspected him.

"So five or six years passed, and we heard nothing of Rachel. In that time I had three children born—those you know. We were backwards and forwards from London so often that I left Rebecca with my mother to manage the shop. By the influence of the Decie's they had made a fair business. Ah! the Meyers; I had almost forgotten them. You will see presently how their jealousy injured me.

"It was about this time that the Captain quarrelled with his brother. It was over money matters, for by this time my master had got into low water; often times he hadn't sufficient to satisfy his debts of honour. Then came one night when he reached home, staggering like a drunken man, with his face like a sheet of paper. When I asked him what was wrong, he just said in a stem, quiet way, we must go to Westport on the morrow, and went to bed.

"So down here we came, and put up at the best hotel in the town. In the afternoon the Captain gave me a note to take to The Moat.

"'On that answer my honour depends,' he said to me.

"Then I knew it was for money, and to The Moat I went. They showed me into Sir Percival's study, where he was writing.

"He read the note through without so much as a change of eyelid, then appeared undecided. After reading the letter again he went out, leaving me alone.

"He was away some time, so to pass the moments I fell to looking round the place. In the wall was an iron safe with the door open, and in there, lying open, was a diamond necklet. Ah! you know what an eye a Jew has for precious stones. Just as I was wondering what the worth of it was Sir Percival came back.

"'Tell your master the answer is 'no,'" he said.

"I should have gone then, only, as ill-luck would have it, Lady Decie came in. I could see that her face was disturbed and uneasy, for as Sir Percival looked at her he shook his head. Presently they got whispering together, she asking some favour, he looking determined. With a look at me she beckoned him out, and then I don't know how it was, but a moment later the diamond necklet was in my pocket."

The speaker paused, his head bent forward in a listening attitude, for in the distance there was a subdued murmur of voices. He slipped on his heavy boots and rose to his feet.

"It's nothing," said Speedwell, impatiently. "Go on."

"I don't know. Sometimes the shadows frighten me," the convict resumed. "Well, I'd hardly done it when Sir Percival returned. He seemed annoyed and restless, but he had not changed."

"'I have nothing to add,' said he. 'You have your message.'

"I was glad enough to go now. When I told the Captain, he just whistled softly, and looked away from me. Then making bold, I asked him how much he wanted to save him.

"'I can't go back to London without 500,' he says.

"It didn't take me long to make up mind. I knew we hadn't half so much money at home, so I determined to try Isha Meyer. When I showed him the bracelet, I saw his eyes shining, but I thought nothing of it then. So the long and short of it was that he agreed to lend me the money, and I was to call again in the afternoon.

"I must have been mad when I did it. So back I went to the Captain, where another surprise awaited me. I heard a sound of voices in the room, so after I'd knocked more than once, I went in, and there was a woman hanging round my master's neck, crying and sobbing. When she heard me she looked round, and

I saw it was my sister.

"That was a nice thing, wasn't it? But no need to say more about that. Woman like, she had scented out danger, and come down post haste to warn him. When he had explained all round it was late in the afternoon. As I was starting to Meyer's again there came a knock at the door, and in walked a couple of policemen and old Meyer himself. Directly I caught sight of his face, grinning and chuckling, I knew I was lost. It was awful luck. It appears that the necklet had a peculiar fastening, and Meyer, being a skilled workman, had been once employed to mend it. He spotted it in a moment, and directly my back was turned must have posted over to The Moat and seen Sir Percival. That was his revenge. Mine will come.

"I need not say any more. My mother would have found the money, the Captain would have begged me off on his knees, but Sir Percival was adamant. I was tried and convicted, and sentenced to ten years' penal servitude. But my time will come, boy. Every day, every month, every year has added to my hate, till it has become a disease. You will have to help me. I can wait; but the time is coming, and then, Sir Percival, and then——"

Behind the mask of night the convict's face was painted with a black malignant hate. The memory of his wrongs had been cherished till they formed part of his being.

He murmured to himself in his short unkempt beard.

"And how do you know this man was my father?" Speedwell asked.

"Because you bear your mother's assumed name. But mind, that secret is yours and mine. Some day I will tell you how I recognised you for certain. And mind, if you tell Rebecca who you are she will turn you from the door, though you are dying of hunger. There is one thing no Jew ever forgives, and that is love for one of them to a Christian. Your mother could have brought no deeper degradation on her race and name than she did. Even I would have seen her in a coffin first. That noise again?"

It seemed like the softened tread of footsteps; as if the shadows were marching on them in ghostly squadrons. There was a sudden silence, till a bright light flashed out in one long dazzling streak.

"Saul Abrahams, I arrest you in the Queen's name!"

There was a quick rush forward, a sound of a pistol on the startled air, a shimmer of blue, and the quick twinkle of silver buttons. A short struggle, and the iron bands closed on the convict's wrists.

Speedwell stood amazed for a moment, then a hand was laid upon his arm, and a voice whispered, "Into the water—quick. Do not be afraid, I will follow you."

It was not in his nature to be afraid. Under cover of the darkness he slid into the black inky pool striking out, and as he did so his course was guided by an unseen hand. A moment later he was standing on the further bank.

"Who is it?" he whispered.

The unseen hand, still resting on his arm, drew him away towards the town. So they walked on silently till the light began to grow bolder in the distance. Speedwell glanced at his companion's face. It was Miriam.

"What brings you here?" he cried.

"Your danger. I heard you steal down the stairs and followed you. Something told me where you were going. Tell me, is that man——"

She said no more, but completed her sentence with a backward swing.

"You have repaid me for what I have done for you," he said. "Promise me that what you have seen to-night shall never be repeated—promise. The man I was with is your father."

IV –

Though Speedwell's exhortation to silence was conceived in best intent, it proved to be of no avail. And as he lay through the night, watching the pallid stars fade from the infinite scroll of heaven, till morn came up from the east, like the outstretched wings of a bird, and the mast needles 'gan to line the morning mists, he travelled in imagination the old weary journey. The Jewish blood ran in his veins. That was the barrier between him and the Christian race. Moreover, Abraham's words had made a deep impression upon him. He, too, felt the mysterious tie of consanguinity which binds the chosen people together. And his mother had received the greatest wrong of all from a Gentile. Henceforth he was a Jew.

Idle Westport, standing out of doors in the morning sun—listless, sullen, discontented, with brooding hate lurking in every hollow eye and haggard cheek—heard the news. Some had gathered round the police court, that magnetic focus of attraction for the unemployed, deriving some scant comfort, as Rochefoucauld says, from the contemplation of other's misfortunes. Presently, passing through the idlers to the Magistrate's room, came Sir Percival Decie. Haughty and listless; clean, spotless, immaculate; as different to the common clay as man could be—and as he passed a murmur ran round, for the county magnate was far from popular; a common thing for a country gentleman who has a profound contempt for the masses and a passion for preserving game. A deadly foe of poachers, therefore.

There was not much business upon the paper, Presently Saul Abraham was placed in the dock. Calmly he looked round the rugged assembly, then fixed his glittering eyes upon the chairman, with a glance of bitterest hate and enmity.

"I merely ask for a remand, your worship," said the chief of police, after the preliminaries had been gone through. "The prisoner is arrested on suspicion of being one Saul Abrahams, who has been missing from Portland Gaol for the past few weeks."

Sir Percival looked at the prisoner through his gold-rimmed spectacles. The name seemed to strike him in some vague way as a familiar one. But he folded his white hands judicially, waiting for the witness to continue.

In the background Miriam and Speedwell stood together. The lad was watching the proceedings with languid interest, like one who has witnessed kindred sights before. Miriam remained quietly by, her face pale as marble, though no sign of inward emotion escaped her; it was too terribly real; so hideously patent for anything but dumb fascination.

The prisoner there was her father—that rugged, haunted-looking wretch, with the wild eyes and dark, evil face. Once he turned towards her with a scowl, their eyes meeting. In spite of her natural courage, her limbs trembled, and she sank back into the listless, patient crowd.

"What will they do with him?" she whispered, at length.

Speedwell turned to her, striving to recollect the small amount of criminal lore, most of which he had learnt by experience, but any answer of his was rendered unnecessary. Abrahams spoke for himself. The charge had been read over to him. The angry multitude waited in dreary anticipation for him to speak.

"No use denying it," he said; "I am the man, Sir Percival Decie." He folded his arms, looking defiantly before him. "You ought to know me."

Sir Percival looked over his gold spectacles in haughty amazement. For a moment the sheer audacity of the words amazed him.

"Don't you know me?" he screamed in a passion of despair. "Don't you know the man you persecuted? Saul Abraham, the thief, the gaol-bird, the man who robbed you."

The indifferent audience were aroused now. An electric thrill seemed to go through them, as they bent together, whispering to one another. Scarcely had they time to bring recollection to bear, for most of them remembered the convict now, before he had disappeared from the dock. Sir Percival, red and hot, was smoothing his ruffled dignity by a liberal use of handkerchief, and wearing his severest judicial aspect. To his mind the majesty of the law had been most grossly outraged.

Miriam fought her way through the throng, her eyes glittering, her face aflame. She heard nothing of the jeers and mocking laughs which followed her. So fast did she go that Speedwell, struggling behind, was barely emerging from the court before she was half way down the street. With a few rapid strides he was by her side.

"Don't take on!" he whispered. "Don't let them see you feel it!" There was something stirring his pulses—a reckless courage which cast out fear. "Try and smile, Miriam! You cowardly wretches!"

But had the whole world been laid at Miriam's feet she could not have uttered a single word. Shame and indignation choked her; the reckless laughter of the crowd sounded in her ears like a horrid nightmare. To the spectators in their misery it was good to see a fellow-creature in distress, and a new zest was added to their sport by the fact of her being one of the hated Jews. But, reckless as they were, there was something in her manner which protected her from bodily hurt.

"I can't understand it!" she gasped, at length. "How—how do they know——"

"That he is your father? Easily enough. Many of them remember now who had forgotten; besides, disgrace travels quickly. What is that?"

The crowd became more dense, there was a tramp of heavy footsteps, and suddenly Miriam and her champion found themselves forgotten. The girl began to recover herself, and, looking round, saw that Sir Percival Decie himself standing by her side, holding a boy by the hand. His face had lost its judicial severity; he looked somewhat anxious, and glanced uneasily at the lad by his side.

Miriam drew herself away, as if afraid of contact with some unclean thing. But Sir Percival did not notice this, for his glance was riveted on the procession coming along the street.

First came some score of workmen walking in military order, and carrying stout sticks gaily decorated with ribbons; then followed a cart, and seated therein were four men, evidently conscious of their own celebrity, for they assumed a ludicrous air of importance, which ill-accorded with their grimy garments and coarse, repulsive countenances.

They were drawn along amidst cheers and tumult, which waxed hotter as the crowd passed along, gathering like a snowball. Miriam turned a white, scared face to Sir Percival, who was pale as herself.

"What is it?" Speedwell asked, listlessly. "Fortunate for us, anyway."

"Poachers!" Miriam whispered. "Ah! I forgot you can't understand. These men were sentenced to four months' imprisonment for poaching on Sir Percival Decie's land. The hands made a great deal of it at the time, for it seems some of them were starving. They will kill him if they see him."

Speedwell glanced at the Baronet in his turn, feeling a perfect callousness as to his fate.

"It will do him good to be hustled about a bit," he said. "I suppose he has feelings like us common people."

"You don't know what you are saying," cried Miriam. "You don't know these men—I do. Oh, pray that they do not see him!"

As if in answer to this outspoken prayer, a hoarse murmur suddenly shot up to the silent sky, like the roar of surf upon a rock-bound shore. Like the waves thereon, the multitude swayed and broke, as they surged towards Sir Percival and his youthful companion. The sense of wrong and misery had fired their blood like wine; they were mad for vengeance now, mad and ruthless as the mob which bore Louis Capet to the scaffold.

Sir Percival's hat had fallen off in the first rush, so he stood facing his wild antagonists bareheaded, his gray hair shining in the bright sunlight. He had stepped back against a high factory wall, and almost unconsciously Miriam and Speedwell had retreated with him. Then they seemed to feel, as the mob felt, that there was a common cause between them.

He is a bold man who in the broad light of day first sets hands upon a fellow creature. There was a certain hesitation now, an ominous lull in the tumult, each waiting for the other to lead the attack. The little group were pale and breathless, but they were not afraid. Perhaps it was this and Sir Percival's haughty look which tamed the fiery passions for awhile. Then someone in the crowd threw a stone, which struck Miriam on the lip and cut the tender flesh, leaving a red stain trickling down her chin.

She scarcely seemed to feel the pain. The blood running in her veins was the life's fluid of a race inured to insult and pain. She took the stone in her hand and cast it back into the crowd with all the strength of her firm right arm. A roar went up again, not wholly anger, for the action was a superbly disdainful one, and commanded admiration. Then almost before the mob could recover, a huge door was opened in the wall, and, as if by magic, their victims disappeared from their gaze.

It was to Speedwell's nimble wit that they owed their safety. While they had been facing the mob he had been casting about for some means of escape. He had climbed to the top of the wall, and, to his delight found they were only a few yards from the folding doors, bolted now since the factory was closed. To slip down and draw the bolts, leaving the door to be pushed open, was the work of a moment, and almost before he was missed he was back again. Inch by inch he had edged the little party, till they stood against the door. Suddenly pushing it back, he quickly got them through. When the mob rushed for the door it was fast as bolts and bars could bind it.

It was a large factory-yard they found themselves in, silent as the grave, save for the murmurs from behind the wall. Sir Percival turned to his companions with unruffled dignity.

"I have to thank you," he said. "Had it not been for your ready wit I might have been seriously discomposed."

"There is no time to lose!" Miriam cried, cutting short what promised to be a long tirade of courtly thanks. "Some of them will scale the wall, and then we shall be in a worse plight still. Make for the other door before they can get round. Come this way—quick!"

There was no time to lose. Already several grimy, evil faces began to show over the gate. Opposite was another entrance, barred in a similar manner, and to this the fugitives made, fortunately reaching it before the first pursuer found his way into the foundry-yard. Turning into the street again, they saw part of the mob had come round to meet them.

"We must run!" Miriam cried. "There is no help for it. Come!"

Sir Percival groaned. The idea of a magnate of his position and standing running bareheaded down the purlieus of Westport was by no means inviting; but, deeming discretion to be the better part of valour, he joined the others as swiftly as his dignity and weight would allow.

They were barely in time, but Miriam knew her way. A few moments later they found themselves safe from pursuit in the little dingy shop, into which not the most daring of the mob cared to penetrate.

"To whom am I indebted to this kindness?" Sir Percival inquired, as soon as he had sufficient breath to speak. "Really, had it not been for you, I think—I actually think—they would have laid hands upon me."

Speedwell, no respector of persons, laughed aloud; but Miriam turned away and was silent. For the first time she realised what she had done—how she had risked life perhaps for the deadliest enemy.

"I will tell you, Sir Percival Decie. This is Saul Abraham's house; the child you are speaking to is his daughter. Explain this, sir. Tell me why you bring your hated presence here?"

Rebecca was speaking. Her face was stern and set, her eyes hard and merciless.

The hatred of a decade of years trembled in her voice, for the old wound had been reopened. It was easy to see that she had heard. Sir Percival would have spoken, but Miriam waved him back with a gesture, before which even he was fain to stand aside. In a few words she told the story. The silence became painful, for the voices in the distance had died away.

"So you had to beg your life at the hands of my child," Rebecca said. "It is well, Sir Percival. That should hurt your proud soul. But the time will come when you shall ask for it again and be refused. You have seen my husband this morning. I am told you are master now."

"Really this dramatic display is quite unnecessary," Sir Percival replied, laying some gold upon the counter. "If it is a matter of payment——"

Rebecca swept the coins upon the floor with a disdainful gesture.

"Payment," she cried—"payment for a broken heart, a disgraced home! Rather would we have had a little of your so-called Christian charity."

They stood looking at each other in puzzled silence, the only sound to break the stillness being the tap of Abishai's crutch as he moved about, picking up the glittering coins.

"I see no need to prolong this interview," Sir Percival replied. "You will take neither thanks or money. I can only tender them again. Come, Victor."

The boy, who had been watching the scene intently, turned towards his father. For a moment he hesitated, then held out his hand to Miriam. Her eyes were moist, her lips quivering. In a sudden impulse she put up her mouth, which he kissed tenderly. To him it was nothing; to her an evidence of friendship and sincerity, destined to bear good fruit after many days. A moment later they were gone.

"Miriam," said Rebecca, "is that how you show your hatred?"

"Perhaps I have none to show; perhaps I am wrong to think the disgrace was of our own making," she answered. "You bid me hate Sir Percival and all his kith and kin, but if you had asked me to love the lad it would have been a far easier task."

V - THE SWEET REPUBLICAN

On the incense-burdened air, odorous from Nature's spicy breathings, there floated a babble of melody, falling like a plummet from the heavens, as a lark sailing upwards brimmed over with the music of his soul. Like a wide-spreading sheet of glimmering jewels the sea stretched away into the faint, luminous distance, silent and lonely, save where the sun lingered on a far-off sail, and flushed it with a golden glory, or a white-winged gull flashed like a silver scimitar against the boundless blue. The tiny waves, curled in breaking upon the velvet sands, splashing the rocky sentinels, impervious to storm or tempest as they had been for generations. Seven years had been a brief day in their long lives. So quiet was it there that it seemed hard to believe in the smoking chimneys and roaring furnaces of Westport, only four miles away, except when you turned from the ocean contemplation inland to look towards the drifting pall behind.

It was so quiet and beautiful there on this perfect summer afternoon that one might have felt inclined to wonder that no one had chosen the fair seclusion of the hoary rocks for idle contemplation. But there were two people there gazing seaward and hidden from human ken, as was but natural, for they were lovers, and her head rested upon his shoulder, whilst his arm was round her waist. They seemed like someone we have seen before, alike and yet different, till we realize that seven years ago Hazael Abraham must have been younger than he looks now.

It was a handsome face in a bold fashion, such a people as Murello loved to delineate, dark and swarth, but bearing no trace of that greed, or avarice, or worldliness which manhood sometimes brings. His companion was slighter and fairer, with but little trace of her genealogy upon her features—all beautiful now from the lovelight in her eyes.

"I should like to know," said Hazael, at length, with the air of one who has taken up a broken thread, "where it is going to end, Aurora."

Aurora Meyer, for it was she, smiled dreamily. There was such an infinite content in the present; the world seemed so far off. 'Juliet,' when she pleaded with her lover for a few moments more, never more completely forgot the traditions of her race than this lovelorn damsel now.

"I don't know," she laughed; "I don't care. I have forgotten Westport, and I have you. I am intoxicated with the champagne of Nature; I cannot think."

"I have always been trained," Hazael pursued, didactically, "to hate certain persons, but I must have learnt my lesson badly. First of all, it is Sir Percival Decie and his son Victor. He and I are the best of friends. Then your people. It is certainly true that I don't like them."

"And I don't like yours," replied Aurora; "so there we are quits."

Hazael laughed, as in duty bound, and turned to contemplate his companion's glowing face. It was strange, he thought, that in spite of all his rigid training, with dislike and loathing so carefully inculcated, that he should be here now with the daughter of an hereditary foe by his side, and love for her in his heart. In idle speculation, now, he traced back the hours from the time when acquaintance had developed into friendship, and friendship into admiration. The secret meetings like this one now, stolen with a few bright hours from the leaden casket of Time, the brightest moments of youth and passion.

"They must know some time," he continued; "the question is, when? It will be a hard day for us, but I have friends who will help me. Besides, I shall have Miriam upon my side."

"Can you count upon her?" Aurora asked, with some eagerness. "For your sake will she ever care for me? It is years since we have spoken, but I have always admired your sister, Hazael. She has power?"

"She has more influence than anyone in the house; more, a great deal, than Abishai, in spite of his money. My—my father would have taken possession of everything if it had not been for her."

"She is very beautiful," Aurora answered; "but so stern."

"No; not that, but she is just. Sometimes I feel almost afraid of her; and yet she would do anything for me. If I were to tell her how we stand, that we are man and wife, she would look at me with those great scornful eyes of hers, but she would guard me from danger if she could."

Aurora shivered a little, conscious of some uneasy feeling. The lark had ceased his melody, and fallen sheer from the hazy sky; a thin track of cloud, gossamer as a bridal veil, had trailed across the sloping sun; a low moan came whispering over the silver sea.

"I hope there will be no danger," she said, quietly; "though I am afraid at times. You are a man, and cannot understand these things. But sometimes, when I have not seen you for a day or two, I get uneasy and restless, and then every sound makes my heart beat. Besides, I am afraid of Ruth."

"Poor Ruth!" Hazael laughed. With the unconscious audacity of youth, which sees nothing admirable in common things, the plain elder sister was always an object for languid pity. "Poor Ruth! And what have you need to fear with her?"

"I may be wrong," replied Aurora; "it may be fancy only; but I think she knows. I have watched her carefully."

"But she would say nothing for your sake. Surely, a sister——"

"Hazael, listen to me." She laid her hand upon his arm, a deep flush upon her face as she spoke. "I may be wrong in telling you what I am going to tell you now. In that book of poems you lent me I read of many things I was ignorant of before. There was a play called 'The Mourning Bride.' I liked that so well that I read it through. I was thinking of Ruth at the time, wondering what had come between us lately, when I came across a line which struck me strangely. Would you like to know?"

"If you will tell me—yes. But what has that to do with us?"

"Listen. The line was 'Hell hath no fury like a woman scorned!'"

Hazael glanced into Aurora's flushed face with a look of purest astonishment. For a time he failed to grasp the spirit of the words. Then, as it flashed upon him, the scarlet in Aurora's features was reflected in his own.

"Impossible!" he cried. "She never sees me. I have not spoken to her for years."

"Nevertheless, I am right. You do not know Ruth as I do; how passionate she is, and what headstrong fancies she takes. I do not think she could love purely and suffer for love's sake. It would rather be a blind, wilful passion."

"But, consider, dearest, what you are saying. In the first place, we are strangers, though we have many kindred ties. Oh! it is impossible."

"I may as well tell you all," said Aurora, with some hesitation. "I have become so accustomed to deceit now that I am constantly looking for it in others. And this fancy has taken such a hold upon my imagination that I felt bound to try it. When Ruth and I are alone together I talk of you—I mention your name suddenly. Ah! you should see the effect it has. One night, in her sleep, she spoke your name, 'Hazael,' softly, just like this. I am mistaken? Would that I could think so."

"It is flattering enough, no doubt, but somewhat alarming, too," said Hazael, ruefully. "In my wildest dreams I never expected this. But, after all, she is your sister; and, besides, if she has taken a fancy for me, she will doubtless act the part of the self-denying heroine of the story book."

"Unfortunately Ruth is not a story book heroine, but a hot-blooded, passionate woman," Aurora replied, cynically. "All our lives we have not been drawn together as sisters usually are; there are few ties of sympathy between us."

"But do you think Ruth actually suspects?"

"I am afraid so; I am afraid of being followed and discovered. Every day it seems to be harder for me to get away—some obstacle is placed in the way. Oh, Hazael, cannot you see some way out of the difficulty?"

Hazael calmed these rising fears, chasing the shadows away by soothing words and caresses, sweet and fresh enough in themselves, but the same for all times and ages. Not that he felt too easy in his own mind, for, say as you will, stolen pleasures have a certain bitter mingled with the sweets.

"I suppose Abishai would not help you?" Aurora asked, doubtfully.

"For value received, perhaps,"—with a faint sneer; "only, unfortunately, I have nothing of value to tender for his services. I don't think it would be any exaggeration to say that Abishai would do anything for money. It is a nice reputation for a young man he has—the Westport miser. It seems hard that I should be so poor, and he worth thousands. Speedwell, again——"

"I hate that man!" Aurora exclaimed, with a shiver. "I often wonder if he has any heart. What Miriam can see in him——"

"Much the same that we do," Hazael answered, dryly. "You don't suppose she cares for the fellow; not but what he would do anything for her, but she is meet for better men than he."

There was a long silence again. The waves came rolling in close to the giant rocks, throwing foamy wreaths of spray over the brown seaweed, which swayed in the translucent water like a tangle of snakes at play. The sun slanted over the distant waters far away behind a glowing tract of rose pink and deep orange gold, save where a sail had crossed the shining pathway, where it lingered, a dull, blood-red spot, upon the radiant glory. From the sloping cornlands behind came a faint wailing call as the glossy crows whirled up wildly from the fields of emerald grain.

There was with it all a stillness which invited sympathy and confidence; the hour and time when heart goes out to heart, and all things artificial are forgotten.

The sun lay full upon Aurora's face, bathing it in a flood of light till it seemed something etherial and almost holy.

"It cannot last like this," she said, partly to herself.

"I know it," Hazael answered, practically. "But what can I do? My employers at the bank might raise my salary, particularly if Mr. Lockwood would say a good word for me. Perhaps I have never told you that it is a rule with them that a clerk shall not marry until his income reaches a hundred and fifty pounds a year. I fear sometimes that we have been too hasty, Aurora. We might have been more patient."

"I would have waited," the girl answered, with a drooping lip. "Remember, that is what I asked for. You are not sorry?"

"No, no," Hazael hastened to reply; "surely not. I am blaming myself for the selfishness I have shown. My darling, I would not undo it if I could."

Aurora's face lightened with a pleased smile. The sun was still upon her, but now the golden flush was tinged with a faint pink hue. For a moment she hesitated, as if about to speak in spite of failing courage.

"I am glad to hear you say that," she murmured, "because it gives me confidence. Hazael, have you never wondered, have you never anticipated anything beyond our own happiness—nothing else, but love?"

"And a cottage, as the man says in the play, with bread and cheese to commence with. Is that what you mean?"

"A cottage, yes. And did it never strike you that in our home, when it does come, that we shall not always be alone?"

"Go on," said Hazael, quietly. His words were low, but there was something in his throat which seemed to rise up and choke him. "But tell me all."

"I would not tell you that until I was certain. Now I know. If we were together and could face the world, it would make me happy, but I cannot tell what to do now. Two months is not long."

Hazael made no reply. He watched the sun's red rim dip below the golden waters, and die in a bath of glory, but he saw nothing there. Aurora never took her eyes from his face, striving to read something of comfort or seeing sympathy.

VI - WELL MET

Signor Sartori, professor of magnetism and electro-biology, lounged along the street with a semi-professional swagger, the effect of which was somewhat marred by the dilapidated condition of his boots. The house of entertainment he was in search of was not precisely one noted for fashion or elegant appointments, but it had the virtue of cheapness, and the professor's exchequer was at ebb.

The Blue Dragon was a low, beetling house, with an overhanging upper storey, a small bar for the better class of customers on the one side, and a common tap upon the other. The landlord, an obese personage, bearing upon his interesting countenance the mark of his affection for his own wares, had once been a notorious poacher; indeed, no one less than one of the celebrities whose triumphant progress through the streets of Westport had nearly proved so disastrous to Sir Percival Decie. Virtue, to use the old copy-book precept is its own reward; but Mr. Joseph Ingram had found it something more. To him it represented popularity, and popularity found its vent in a public house, which was not viewed with particular favour by the guardians of the law.

Signor Sartori walked into the bar with as great a clash as the thinness of his boot heels would allow. His presence did not seem particularly pleasing to the proprietor, who was seated in his shirt sleeves imbibing strong waters.

But the professor was not the man to be deterred by any show of taciturnity, for he ordered a pint of beer, adding that the widespread fame of that liquid had induced him to travel thither from afar.

"Some likes beer, some has a fancy for swipes," returned the landlord, unbending a little: "but you gets none but the best here, and the price is four-pence."

"The price, my good man, is a detail," returned the Professor, waving his hand loftily—"a mere sordid detail. However, there it is. Short reckonings make long friends, a maxim I adhere to religiously; it is part of my philosophy, and 'sile et philosophus esto.' You understand."

The proprietor nodded, as if the Latin tongue held no enigma for him; besides which, the stranger's sentiments were sound, and summed up in one word the whole duty of man as interpreted between thirsty mankind and a landlord. The scientific speaker had not dropped his quotation without calculating upon its effect. He knew full well the reverent admiration the lower classes have for 'book learning,' and, moreover, no disciple of Lavater could class Mr. Ingram as a ripe scholar.

"Stranger in these parts, I reckon?" he ventured.

"In these parts, yes. I came here 'illotis manibus,' and, ahem! I am in the fashion. But first, by your leave, we will discuss a little business. I suppose I can have a bed here."

"You can have anything by paying for it," was the jocular reply, not entirely void of any transient suspicions. "Got any traps?"

"I can have anything by paying for it," mused the professor. "Truly a logical remark; not altogether innocent of self-interest, but still a fact. My traps have not arrived; they are too vast to be dragged about the country. But money, my dear sir—money is more tangible."

Saying this, he threw half a sovereign upon the table with the air of a man to whom such coins were plentiful, not to say abundant. The landlord's face lightened so far as its purple hue would allow, as he tested the metal with his teeth. There was no longer ground for suspicion.

"Perhaps you would like a bit of supper?" he asked.

"Presently, my good sir—presently. Catch then, oh, catch the transient hour. Improve each moment as it flies. Business before pleasure—a motto I never lose sight of. Ah! but for that golden maxim, I should never have held the proud position it is my good fortune to hold now."

For a moment he seemed lost in the contemplation of his own grandour. In reality he was threshing about in his brain to find some way of leading the conversation in the channel he desired. Presently he came back to mundane things with a faint sigh. He took the end of a cigar from his pocket, and, lighting it, blew out a cloud of smoke.

"But even in my case there are times when I weary of popularity," he resumed. "One gets sick of public adoration and flattery. Gradually, but surely, the sword is wearing out the scabbard. I must—in duty to myself, I must retire. Even in the giddy throng, courted and flattered by ladies of high degree, I sigh for the green fields and babbling brooks. In the gilded saloon I long for the murmur of the sea, and turn satiated from contemplation of priceless treasures."

"I dare say you've seen a mort o' plate in your time," murmured the landlord, quite overcome by this dazzling diatribe, "and diamonds."

"Sick of them, for after all what are they beside nature's peerless jewellery?"

The landlord shook his head gently. The reminiscences of sundry journeys in search of valuables in his early life rose up before him. Here was a man who had distinctly wasted a priceless opportunity.

"But more of that anon," pursued the Professor. "Like Cincinnatus returned to the plough, so I sigh for the country. I should like to buy a little place in this beautiful neighbourhood. There was one house as I came along which struck me with admiration. About four miles out close to the sea; bosomed in hanging woods, and washed by the changing waves. Ah!"

"The Moat you mean," returned the landlord, practically. "Sir Percival Decie's place. Nice enough, too, for them as likes the country."

"A county magnate, I presume," Signor Sartori answered, leaning his head back with eyes fast closed. "Enviable mortal. Has he any family?"

"One son only, and a good one, mind. None of your 'aughtiness like his father. Got a good word for everyone. More like his uncle, they say."

"And who might this delectable uncle be?"

"I don't know nothing about delect'ble," replied the host, sulkily. "All I know is he made himself scarce fifteen years ago. Not but what I can remember him to be a fine dashing young fellow before he got into trouble, and had to go away to foreign parts for the benefit of his health."

"Was there anything the matter with his health?" asked the Professor, anxiously.

"Not as I knows of, captin'. They did say close confinement wouldn't be good for him. But it's an old story now. Saul Abrahams was the name of his valet. A Jew he was, and Saul managed to get himself into gaol over it, but the Captain, he got off."

"And was very likely the biggest scoundrel of the two. That's the way of the world, Mr. Ingram—the way of the world. Did you ever hear anything of this valet again?"

"Once he broke prison eight years ago now, and was taken back. Next time they took more care of him, but he's out now, and been in Westport here a matter of six months or more."

"Ah," said the Professor with a deep breath—"ah! Most interesting to a student of human nature, but dry. Suppose you fill our glasses again."

To this invitation the landlord acceded with an alacrity surprising in one of his solid proportions. By the time he had returned the guest had taken from his pocket a pack of cards, which he spread on the rough table before him, and went through a dazzling evolution of stage conjuring in a manner which fairly won the admiration of the spectator.

For some time this continued, till the sound of a footstep coming along the flagged passage fell upon their ears. Signor Sartori placed his cards in his pocket again and resumed his old airy attitude. The new-comer was a man of perhaps sixty years of age, his long black hair plentifully besprinkled with gray. His face was lined and scarred; heavy with that shrinking, sullen look which marks a man who has come in contact with the law; a little defiant, too, but showing the shame stamped there. The landlord nodded distantly, the new-comer carelessly, as he flung himself into a seat. Close behind him, as if afraid or ashamed to be recognised, there followed a young man dressed in the height of modern fashion, and wearing a profusion of jewellery; though his general appearance had that indescribable appearance of caricature which a man has who is not to the manner born. He was handsome in a florid way, with good bold features and regular teeth; but his eyes were shifty and his mouth thin and cruel looking. To him the surly landlord turned with something like respect.

"A fine evening, Mr. Speedwell," he said, rubbing his hands together.

Speedwell, for he it was, nodded shortly, and turned a languid, supercilious glance in the direction of the professor, who, with eyes closed and hat drawn over his face, was reclining against the greasy wall.

"We are honoured to-night," he said. "Who is the dilapidated stranger, Ingram?"

The master of magnetism opened his eyes, looking languidly around. Presently his eyes fell fall upon Speedwell's face, where they remained, looking him through and through in a long, concentrated stare. Despite his assurance, he could not return the steady gaze.

"You seem to imagine we have met before?" he asked, insolently.

"Well, yes," said the Professor, cheerfully, "I really think we have, though doubtless such a gentleman—and anyone can see you were that—has but little in common with a dilapidated stranger—for that expression much thanks. I have a good memory for faces. It is so long since we met that I have forgotten whether it was Exeter or Manchester Gaol."

Speedwell stepped forward with his hand upraised; but there was a look in the philosopher's eyes which checked the rising outburst of passion. A ghastly smile spread over his features, as if perforce he enjoyed the joke. It was well, he thought, to keep a rein upon his feelings, for one never knows how the mistakes of a past life will rise up in judgment against us.

Abraham had listened in rapt attention, his glass partly raised to his lips, where it remained as if he had been suddenly turned to stone.

"You seem to have an extensive acquaintance with prisons," said Speedwell, his lips trembling, and a red spot burning on either cheek. "I trust your apprenticeship has been a profitable one."

"Enough to enable me to tell a scoundrel when I see him!" the Professor answered.

Speedwell laughed.

"You are calculated to judge, no doubt," he retorted. "A fellow feeling makes us wondrous kind. Ingram, come this way."

With this Parthian shot, Speedwell swaggered from the room with an assumption of ease which he was far from feeling. The landlord followed, leaving his strange guest staring at Abraham, who had remained in precisely the same attitude with his glass raised partly to his lips. The professor gazed fixedly at his companion with the same enigmatical smile.

"Well," he said, at length—"well, Saul Abraham, and what now?"

"If it had been a hundred years," Abraham answered, vaguely, in his husky tones, like one who speaks in a dream—"if it had been ten hundred years, I should have known that voice. I have prayed for this day—me, a poor, sorrowful scoundrel!—and my prayer has been granted. I knew him when others didn't—I knew him directly." His voice broke down to a long wavering quaver, like the strings of some instrument out of tune. "Oh, master, master! to think of you coming home like this, and knowing me after all these years!"

He burst into tears like a child, and, falling by the stranger's side, seized upon his hand, mumbling over it as a faithful dog might do. He smiled still, but his eyes were moist. When he spoke again, his voice seemed more commanding and a little contemptuous.

"Abraham, does it strike you that you are making a consummate ass of yourself?"

Abraham rose to his feet obediently, still holding the other's hand, as if afraid that he might lose him. It was strange to see how this hard scoundrel was moved by the sound of his once master's voice.

"My dear master—my dear master—Captain——"

"No no; not that!" Trevor Decie—for he it was—exclaimed, sharply. "I—I have forfeited that title long ago. Besides," he continued, in a kinder voice, "I am master of yours no longer. I am Signor Sartori now; and, harkee, not a word of this to a soul."

Abraham bowed his head meekly. He was calm now, though his hands shook a little.

"You do not despise me, like the rest?" he asked.

"God knows I don't. What right have I to do so?"

"I hate them all, and they hate me. But it does one good to hear a pleasant voice again, and yet I have reason enough to loathe the sound of your name. But I can't. You will always be master to me."

"Sorry I can't congratulate you upon a better," Decie returned, with a touch of cynicism. He was his natural self now. "Sit down and tell me all the news. I have heard nothing of Westport for years. If my brother——"

"That's no part of the contract," Abraham interrupted, scowling. "Mind, what I do for you. I do willingly; but as for him——But no matter, sir. A time will come—a time is coming now—when Sir Percival Decie shall cry quits."

"It must be extremely fatiguing keeping your wrath warm all these years,"

Decie observed, with gentle irony. "I trust you will not hurt Sir Percival. But never mind him now. Tell me all the news."

Abraham to the best of his ability obeyed. It was but a brief, uninteresting chronicle, after which the conversation became more personal.

"Your family must be grown up now?" observed Decie, after a pause.

"Yes, and doing well. Abishai—that is the cripple, you remember—has the old place for his business, pawnbroker and money-lender. He is getting rich, too—when a man can keep himself on his savings he soon makes money—and yet I think he would see me starving before he would lend me a sixpence."

"A touching trait of nationality, Saul. You had three children. I think?"

"You are right, sir," Abraham answered, with a pleased smile. "Hazael and Miriam. Ah, she has grown into a rare beauty—a rare beauty!"

"And that interesting specimen of humanity just gone out? That, I hope, for your sake, is not your second son?"

"No, sir," Abraham replied, placidly. "I am sorry to say he is yours."

Throughout the whole of the interview this was the only semblance of a reproach the ex-convict allowed himself to make. But the traditions of race and the remembrance of his own wrongs could not resist this passing sneer.

"I am fortunate indeed," said Decie, bitterly, after a few astonished questions and the necessary answers. "'Par nobile fratrum.' I had not anticipated this. In the course of a tolerably wide experience I have not been in durance vile, but I'll swear that fellow has. I trust he is not acquainted with his exalted patrimony?"

"I can't say he doesn't know who his father is, sir, but he does not know you, which is the great thing. Captain, I never betrayed a secret of yours yet; you don't think I'm going to begin now?"

The captain smoked for a few moments in ruminative silence. He was far too much of a philosopher to be perturbed or long cast down by the discovery he had made.

"I don't think you will," he said. "Now, look here, as I shall probably remain in Westport for some time, we had better come to an understanding. I am not going down on my knees to my relations asking for money. To you, as well as everybody else, I am Signor Sartori, professor of magnetism and electro-biology. I shall go and see my brother presently, and calm his fears. I am not likely to be recognised by anyone here, and probably I shall give a few performances. Mind you, my show is no sham; I have the gift of magnetism. Come here at this time to-morrow night, and I will tell you what to do."

Decie resumed his old jaunty attitude, and turned away from his old servant, for Speedwell had returned. He stood before the fireplace playing somewhat nervously with the numerous pendants to his watch chain, an affectation of a smile upon his face. The mesmerist had risen and lounged in the direction of the door; Abraham would have followed but that an almost invisible motion of his hand bade the other to stay.

"Who is the vagabond," Speedwell asked, irritably. "He has a sharp tongue."

"A mesmerist," Abraham answered, shortly, "travels about the country reading people's thoughts and all that."

"Well! I had almost a mind to give him a trial just now. I should like to see any man who could read my thoughts; he would be welcome to all he would find out."

"Well, I don't know," the ex-convict mused; "I don't know. Depend upon it that it isn't all humbug, and if I were you I should keep away, because you hav'n't got the cleanest conscience as ever was, Mr. Philip Speedwell."

VII - THE SMOOTHER SIDE

Along the bold outline of the North-East Coast it would be hard to find a more perfect residence than The Moat. Down a barricade of steepening rock lay the wide-spreading sands; behind uprose a sweeping woodland, and in the basin thus formed the house lay. Once it had been a grim castle, the walls of which still stood, though the great dining-hall, once resonant with the clank of mail and clatter of arms, now did duty for the stables. The house was cunningly built in the ruins, so that from a distance it was hard to distinguish the place of habitation, as the ancient walls hid the more modern structure from view. Internally the place was modern enough, giving it a peculiarly incongruous look, which was anything but unpleasing. Now, as night had fallen, and the sloping woods cast deep shadows downward, it was easy to perceive the place was inhabited, for lights gleamed out far across the sea, making a beacon and a guide for the fisherboats out upon the German Ocean. There was an air of festivity in these lights, glowing ruddy in every window; a show of plate upon the oaken sideboard in the large dining-room, racing cups and salvers, trophies of prowess by flood and field of Decies long dead and gone. The branching antlers upon the walls gleamed in the soft light of tapers, the claret stood warming in the fender, and the table glittered with china and silver and fragile glass. In the drawing-room, with windows barred and shuttered, as if to keep out the low sob of the tide, was still warmth and brightness. Standing before the fire—for the night was chill—in the typical British attitude, stood Sir Percival. He had aged but little since we saw him last; a little stouter, perhaps, a little more polished about the temples, but prosperity sits easily upon us, and defies, as naught else can do, the onslaught of Time's artillery.

There was another figure, too, half-shaded from the light, seated in a deep armchair, with legs crossed in a comfortable abandonment. Like Sir Percival, he was in evening dress, which set off a fine figure and pleasing face to advantage. Victor Decie was not precisely handsome, but he had an honest, pleasant face, and that peculiar expression, half natural, half educated, which stamps the cast of Vere De Vere. It is hard, says someone, to be mistaken for a gentleman; it would have been harder for Victor to have been confounded with anything else.

Sir Percival laid down his newspaper and looked at his watch—a huge gold affair, with a painted dial—and consulted it carefully.

"They are late!" he exclaimed. "By my time, at least seven minutes."

"Mr. Lockwood is a model of punctuality," Victor laughed—"a virtue he has been trying to impress upon me from childhood's hour. He probably reckons by Westport time. A very different thing to yours."

"That watch never varies," Sir Percival answered, solemnly contemplating the dial—"never! My father would not have carried an unreliable timepiece."

Victor admitted the probity of the invincible time-keeper in question, and listened to the distant crash of wheels which gradually began to rise above the moan of the advancing tide. There was nothing novel in the conversation, it being taken as a kind of grace before meat each evening at The Moat. Presently the door opened, and past the servant came Mark Lockwood, with his daughter on his arm, after the fashion of a bygone generation.

He, too, was much the same as when we saw him last, standing with hands folded behind him, striving to read Speedwell's careless, defiant face. With him it seemed as if time had stood still, indeed as if the clock of hours had been put back, as he stood there, the light shining on his silvery hair, falling round a shrewd, kindly face. He wore an open coat reaching to his knees, a black satin waist-coat, out of which rushed a cascade of laced ruffles. The homespun breeches and hose were changed now for black satin and silk, with light shoes, in which gleamed two paste buckles.

Ida Lockwood, 'sole daughter of his house and heart,' bent her fair head to hide the little smile which trembled in the corners of her mouth. There was a demure look upon her beautiful face, belied by the merry sparkle in her great gray eyes—a fair picture of English girlhood, with the light falling upon her piled-up hair and shimmering white draperies. As he turned with stately courtesy to bid her welcome, Sir Percival relaxed his judicial air, and hastened to restore his watch to its hiding-place.

"The Moat is honoured," he said, gallantly; "and I—what shall I say for myself?"

"Should I choose your compliments?" Miss Lockwood laughed. "I am afraid you think me susceptible to flattery. And yet, probably, five minutes ago you were blaming me for being late."

"Never a happier guess," said Victor. "How did you know that?"

"Nay, friend Decie; but I must contradict thee there," Mark Lockwood interpolated, gently, "for thou'rt wrong. It still wants some moments to the hour of seven."

"This watch has never been known to vary, Victor."

But the latter had taken the opportunity of seating himself by Miss Lockwood's side, leaving the elders to their endless controversy.

"Methinks our young friend hath better employment," said the manufacturer, dryly, "than arbitrating between thou and me. Leave them alone, my friend—leave them alone. Art satisfied?"

"Nothing, my dear Lockwood—nothing could be more to my mind. No one who has known your daughter all these years could fail to admire her beauty of mind and—ah—person. Indeed, a more fitting alliance for my son I could not have chosen. Perhaps at first I was a little inclined to lean towards birth; but trade now-a-days has become so respectable that really——"

The Baronet waved his hand to demonstrate the vast respectability and solid position that commerce has attained.

"That really," said Lockwood, taking up the parable, "thou hast not scrupled to benefit from it thyself. But I much fear thou wilt never succeed in making those iron works pay."

"My dear sir, in time, they must pay. Have I not had the opinion of every expert in the North of England? I am not naturally a sanguine man, which, after all, is only another name for a fool, but I certainly anticipate a large return for the capital I have expended."

Any further discussion upon this point was interrupted by the announcement of dinner at this moment. Sir Percival offered his arm to Miss Lockwood, the others following behind across the flagged hall where the figures stood in armour, and ancient spears rested on the walls. For a time they sat in silence, broken only by the clatter of plates and the insidious whisperings of the well-trained servants as they glided from place to place.

"It is a strange thing, though, that your protege, Speedwell, takes so much interest in my works," Sir Percival commenced, abruptly. "A remarkably shrewd fellow for a young man."

"A deserving youth," replied Lockwood, with his usual readiness to say a kind word, "and a credit to my training. It is not often I make a mistake, friend Decie, as thou know'st."

"I am not so sure of that," Victor put in, meditatively. "Of course, I don't mean to criticize your judgment; but I cannot tolerate that man. I hate a fellow who assumes the gentleman as he does."

"He holds a responsible position for a young man," the Baronet observed; "and I must say he does his duty well. And yet I cannot understand why he did not stay with you, Lockwood."

"It is hard to control ambition," replied Mr. Lockwood, sententiously; "he always had a talent for figures—always. So when he applied for the managership of Armstrong's bank, I could not refuse a reference. And, truly, I must say he worked up a valuable connection. Though I have small occasion to ask favours of my bankers, I have placed my account there."

"And I followed your example—a better one I could not have," Sir Percival observed. "Candidly I do not like these joint-stock banks; one meets with a degree of familiarity there which almost amounts to impertinence."

"I don't like that fellow, Speedwell," Victor said, stoutly. "There is something underhanded in his manner which arouses my suspicions."

Mr. Lockwood shook his head gravely, and deplored this scorning prejudice. Sir Percival was conscious of an uneasy feeling himself, for truth to tell, his commercial speculations had not been productive of much solid satisfaction up to the present, and it was in the power of the manager of Armstrong's bank to make things extremely unpleasant for the master or The Moat.

Iron ore had been found on a piece of outlying property, and it had seemed easy to turn this into money, as many an inexperienced person has thought before. But, instead of this satisfactory outcome, he had found himself, after the lapse of two years, considerably the poorer, and with an overdrawn account to the extent of more than ten thousand pounds.

It was not a pleasant outlook, for he was anything but a rich man. He had always scorned to take advice, and now against the grain, he had decided to enlist the keen intellect and shrewd sense of Mark Lockwood on his side.

Victor turned away from a conversation which to him was distasteful, and devoted himself to the girl by his side. It was much more pleasant to linger there watching her, and listening to the voice of one he loved, than discussing dry details with those who, in the rush and fret of life, had long since lost the glamour and tender recollection of Love's young dream.

Presently, with a laughing challenge, Ida, stole away to the drawing-room, leaving the men to sit over their wine amidst the picturesque confusion the end of a meal always leaves. Scarcely had the sound of her floating dress died away, when Victor rose and followed guiltily. Mark Lockwood nodded to his host with a peculiar smile: the Baronet smiled in return; then the bright look passed away, as he played nervously with his glass.

"Friend Decie, thou hast something of import to say to me?"

"Well, I have," Sir Percival answered, grateful for this abrupt opening, and only too willing to come to the point. "I want your advice."

"Ah, I thought thou wouldst require that sooner or later!" Lockwood laughed. "Said I to myself, he will come to you in good time. So I waited. Go on, friend —take thy time; for surely the young folks will not be pining for our company."

"As you know, I am not a rich man," the Baronet commenced; "nor, as things have turned out, a particularly discerning one. But I did hope to make some money out of the Old Meadow Works, whereas——"

"Whereas you must have lost at least ten thousand pounds."

"How on earth do you know that?" Sir Percival exclaimed.

"Merely my own idea," replied the manufacturer, placidly. "That is about the amount I calculated thou wouldst lose. Thou hast no experience in these things, friend—I have. In other hands, the Old Meadow Works might pay, but not in thine. And this sudden fall in the price of iron, too."

"That is the whole secret of the thing!" cried Sir Percival, eagerly. "At the present moment my capital is lying idle, locked up in metal. Now, supposing we get a sudden rise—supposing this war on the Continent breaks out—what a fortune I shall realize then!"

The sanguine speculator stopped breathless, not only from the rapidity of his own words, but likewise with the contemplation of future splendour. The astute manufacturer smiled, as one might doat the enthusiasm of a child, and, playing with his wineglass, discoursed as if he was speaking to one.

"I am a man of peace, and cannot lend my countenance to unholy strife. But, my friend, has it never struck thee that this war thou'st wishing for may never come? Has it never appeared to thee that this depression is not over yet? And if it lasts, as I fear it will, thy pretty prophecies are likely to cost thee a handsome penny."

"Ah, but you are looking on the darkest side of the question."

"I am looking at it from a business point of view, Sir Percival. Now, listen to me. Thou hast a valuable plant, a valuable stock, but standest in need of more capital. Don't persist in having a continual overdraft at the bank; such things do not inspire credit, and the luxury is an expensive one. Come and see me in business hours, when I can advise thee to the best of my ability. If the works close now it will be a serious loss."

"It will, indeed," said the Baronet, paling visibly; "almost ruin, in fact. Then you advise me to hold on till times are better?"

Mr. Lockwood nodded.

"To use thy capital judiciously—yes. It will be well to raise what is available, even if it is necessary to mortgage thy property. With the men working for thee, and the heavy engagements thou must necessarily have to meet, a sudden call by the bank people would ruin many a far richer man."

Gradually, as he listened, Sir Percival began to understand in what a slough of despond he had cast himself. Thousands of pounds lay locked up in the useless, unsalable iron, cheapening day by day, and heavy liabilities had to be met. As Lockwood's clear, shrewd sense went home to him, he began to see his desperate position. It was possible to raise thirty thousand pounds easily enough, but all this was wanted. He had almost decided to unbosom himself to the manufacturer, when the door opened, and a servant stood there waiting. From the contortions of his usually stolid physiognomy he was struggling from some inward emotion, laughter apparently.

"If you please, Sir Percival, a gentleman wants to see you."

"A gentleman," the Baronet, answered, vaguely, his thoughts far away.

"Leastwise he isn't exactly a gentleman," replied the footman, with a great effort at accustomed gravity; "he's a kind of a man. I particularly told him you could not be disturbed, sir; but before I could interfere he had got into the library, and there he is now as——"

Sir Percival coughed ominously; the servant suddenly came to his senses. It must have been something more than ordinary to cause him to forget his usual good manners.

"Really most extraordinary," observed Sir Percival. "Say I will be with him in a moment; it must be something important. Lockwood, I know you will not mind my leaving you. The claret is at your elbow."

VIII - A PLEASANT SURPRISE

Sir Percival rubbed his eyes to make certain that he would believe their fantastic evidence. He saw a stranger seated before the fire, his long limbs thrown up on each side of the mantelshelf, his body tilted back at the most comfortable angle in an armchair. The Baronet was conscious of a spasm of rage too deep for words, so he fell back, as angry men are apt to do, upon his most withering sarcasm.

"I have not, I believe, the honour of your acquaintance," he said, blandly; "but I beg that you will consider yourself at home."

"A chequered experience of men and things has proved the soundness of your reasoning," the stranger replied—"I have made myself at home. Don't you think you had better take a chair?"

"Your amiability is overwhelming," said Sir Percival, in a choked voice. "As you are so kind I will take a chair." He wheeled round a chair, and sat down, facing the new-comer as well as possible, his hands planted upon his knees, and his face a fine ruby one. "And now, having done so, perhaps you will be good enough to explain this unwarrantable intrusion."

The stranger laughed gently.

"Intrusion is a strong word, sir, and implies a thrusting of one's company where it is neither desirable nor welcome. Now, look at that card, sir—these are my credentials. It is hard, I say—hard for one who has performed before the crowned heads of Europe to be flouted by a mere baronet. And this—to quote Sturt's historic words—this is popularity!"

"It may be a good joke," Sir Percival cried, throwing the unoffending card into the fire; "but I must confess I am too dense to see it. I presume you come here seeking my patronage? After your—your insufferable ignorance of common politeness you will not be surprised if I refuse?"

"On the contrary, my dear sir, I shall be much astonished."

"Indeed! And may I ask how you ground these sanguine expectations?"

"Well," returned the stranger, rising to his feet, and smiling cheerfully, "it is this way: If you refuse to patronise Signor Sartori, he will reluctantly be compelled to abandon the name by which he is known to fame, and appear as Captain Trevor Decie, brother of Sir Percival Decie, J.P., of The Moat, Westport."

The Baronet's inflated dignity collapsed and melted into space like a bubble. He sat upon his seat flabby and dismayed; his jaw hung loose, his face a deep purple, alternately white and haggard.

"I thought you were dead?" he gasped at length.

"And hoped so, too," Trevor Decie replied sardonically; "but objectionable relatives never die; like annuitants they generally live to a green old age. But don't you think, considering that we haven't met for something like twenty years, you might summon up a smile of welcome."

But Sir Percival made no answer. He was far too stunned by this sudden revelation to do anything but gaze feebly in the prodigal's direction, and gasp for breath.

When a man has been fettered all his life to the fetish of British respectability he is prone to look askance at the children of Bohemia. Gradually, as consciousness returned to him, he began to see the hideousness of his position. The sight of his brother was eyesore enough, but that he should be so nearly connected with a professional charlatan who gained a precarious living by stumping the country, was at once a shock and a loathsome surprise.

"This mesmerism business is one of your playful jokes, I suppose?" he asked with feeble hope. "Of course no Decie could really descend to such a thing."

"Out of consideration for the feelings of his ancestors? But let me assure you that I have so far descended. I suppose, even to your unpractical mind, the idea has sometimes occurred to you that I had to live."

Sr Percival groaned.

A private soldier, perhaps even a successful gold-digger, with a long beard and an extensive and peculiar vocabulary of profanity, might have been tolerated, but a low, common-place conjurer!

"Where did you learn your profession?" he asked, feebly.

"When 'Othello' related adventures I believe he had a favourable audience. As I cannot hope for that, may I venture to jog your hospitable faculties. I have no wild yearning to do the prodigal son business, but I have a tender recollection of a certain claret. As a detail perhaps, it is worth mentioning that I have tasted nothing since morning."

Sir Percival rose, and leaving the room, closed the door behind him. When he returned he was bearing with his own hands a neatly-appointed tray, set out with a tempting meal, flanked by a pint bottle of claret.

If he expected to see the prodigal fall to and eat wolfish rapacity, he was mistaken and a little disappointed, for it had occurred to him that if the fallen one was penniless and hungry it would not be a difficult matter to be rid of him at a trifling cost. But the unwelcome guest was too thoroughly cosmopolitan to feel any undue elation. He ate his meal calmly and quietly; even complained in a gentle, deprecatory manner of the sauce, and sipped his claret meditatively.

"I suppose," said Sir Percival, irritated by this display of flagrant ingratitude; for there was little humiliation in his brother's manner—"I suppose—Trevor—that it is not your good fortune to get such a dinner every day?"

"No," replied the Captain, reflectively—"no. When I come to think of it, the cuisine in country hotels is not beyond reproach. There are times when I have to content myself with bread and cheese. But on the other hand, I have my white-letter days. Generally, when in town, I dine at the Langham—perhaps the best place in London. Besides, they know me there, and if I am sometimes short of money,

Quantum nunimorum tantum fidei est.

And my word is my bond.

Besides, there is always the usual remedy."

"I should hardly have suspected that conjuring was so remunerative," the Baronet observed. "From the appearance of your wardrobe I should have thought the contrary."

"Ah! for the present I have fallen upon evil times—no novelty, let me assure you. In a weak moment I decided to give the good people of York the benefit of my ripe experience. But, alas! they refused to believe either in me or my show. Hence it is that you see me in this pitiable condition. A confiding pawnbroker is at present doing duty as my valet; but I never despair. What I lost there I shall find in Westport."

"Do I understand you to mean that you actually contemplate performing as a common mountebank—for that is the only expression—here in Westport almost within earshot of the home of your ancestors?"

"Your metaphor is a trifle mixed," the Professor replied, airily, as he regarded his unhappy brother's fixed stare and forlorn appearance; "but you have grasped my meaning. I am going to perform at Westport. And what is more, my good Percival, you are going to be present."

"Wild horses shall not drag me there," said the Baronet, in a hollow voice. "I am looked up to and respected now; I owe a duty to Society. If any persuasions of mine will induce you to abandon this nefarious, this diabolical scheme, you have them. For the honour of the family——"

"Rot the honour of the family," Trevor Decie exclaimed, in a gust of passion. "Perish such childish babble. What did it ever do for me but place me in a position I was not able to maintain; and when my honour hung on a single thread you refused to hold out a hand to save me from perdition? And you prate to me of family! I come here to-night, after an absence of nearly twenty years, asking and wanting nothing, except that you must patronise my show."

"And if I refuse this modest request?"

"In that case I shall give my entertainment under my own name."

For some moments they stood up glaring at each other—the sleek, well-fed man of wealth and standing, the peripatetic adventurer. Then Trevor Decie turned away with a slight smile.

"It is not worth arguing," he continued, "I shall put your name down upon my bill of course. Pshaw! its no use glaring at me like that; I am not a poor wretch of a poacher who has the misfortune to be brought before you. Sit down."

Sir Percival sat down. He was thoroughly cowed, and felt strangely humiliated by the encounter with this master spirit, and besides which there was after all nothing uncommon in patronising passing talent, and again it would be strange if any Westport people realised the dashing Captain Decie in the professor of electro-biology, Signor Sartori.

"You need have no fear of my being known," the latter said, reading these thoughts; "knowing me as you do now, you will never recognise me when I am upon the stage. And, speaking in confidence, I am no charlatan. I shall show you things which will both astonish and amuse you."

"The mystery to me is why you took up such a line," Sir Percival murmured; "surely there were plenty of other ways of getting a living?"

"You never tried—I have," was the grim reply. "I don't want to refer to old times, but when I went away from Westport on a certain memorable occasion, I got to London, and by dint of selling everything I had, barely managed to save what you humorously term the family honour. Ah," he continued, with a shudder, "I don't want to remember the next three years. I could fill a big volume upon the ups and downs of my life. I have been a waiter in a cheap restaurant, a racing tout, a prompter in a portable theatre. Sometimes, in slack times, I have done 'Othello and Macbeth.' I was a gentleman's valet, till I thought I was recognised by someone in a house where we were staying, and had to bolt. Then I met a ventriloquist and conjurer, and joined him as confederate and factotum. I had an aptitude for that business—plenty of impudence and patter, till gradually I got so used to it that they took me into partnership. Since my old partner died I have been running the show alone, and adding to it bit by bit till I have started on mesmerism and electro-biology. Mind you, that is no sham. I have the natural gift."

"I suppose the fright has influence upon extremely foolish persons?" Sir Percival observed, with a sort of superior amusement.

The electro-biologist smiled, and fixed a pair of glittering eyes upon his brother.

Instantly he became conscious of a peculiar thrilling shock, and a slight tingling sensation in his extremities. The experimentalist took up a glass from the table, and held it out to the other, who took it obediently.

"Now drop it," he said. "Drop it, if you are able to."

But Sir Percival could not obey his own impulse. Strive as he would, the crystal clung to his nervous, locked fingers. Trevor Decie took the glass away, and restored it to the table, and bade the other be seated again.

"That is nothing," he continued, quietly. "Some day I will show you more. I am proud of my powers and fond of my occupation, being naturally restless and a wanderer. But sometimes the home sickness comes upon me, as it has come upon me now. I wanted to see the old place once more, and wondered what you would say to me. Come, Percival; let us be friends again. I am willing to forget the past, if you are. There is my hand. It may have disgraced the lofty traditions of the Decies," he continued lightly, though there was a huskiness in his throat, "but it is honest."

In a moment of feeling, Sir Percival stretched out his hand, which met the other in a warm grip—such a handshake as neither of them had felt for more than twenty years. For a time they were both silent, each winking and blinking at the fire.

"I did not bring any disgrace upon you," the wanderer continued, "and I shall not ask you for anything. For the present I am Signor Sartori and you are my good patron. And now let me hear something about yourself."

In an impulse of confidence, which comes to us all at times, the Baronet laid bare his heart, and told the prodigal everything of interest, even to his difficulty with the new works and their unsatisfactory results. Trevor Decie listened with interest, for in his versatile way he was something of a mechanic, and had more than a passing knowledge of mineralogy. As he listened to the somewhat verbose narrative, he gradually became conscious of the frequent repetition of the name of Speedwell, wondering vaguely where he had heard it before. Then the encounter in the Blue Dragon flashed upon him.

"Who is this Speedwell?" he asked, carelessly.

"Quite a wonderful fellow in his way," Sir Percival answered, his enthusiasm tempered with patronage—"a protege of Lockwood's. You remember Lockwood? Came here quite a youth in rags; Lockwood took him up, and now he is actually manager of Armstrong's Bank. Some say he is a Jew, but I doubt that, for all he lives with those Hebrew people—Abrahams isn't the name? The man was a servant of yours, you remember. He is about here again now; a hardened scoundrel, I hear. But his family have kept themselves respectable— I will say that for their credit—quite respectable; and the oldest is reputed to be well off. Speedwell lives with them."

"Ah," Trevor Decie groaned, "interesting, no doubt; quite the traditional young man, who comes into a thriving place with half a crown in his pocket and dies a millionaire. Sort of things children are taught to read now-a-days."

But the speaker was far from feeling the listlessness and indifference he had for the moment assumed. With knowledge, and knowing that Speedwell had such good cause to hate the name of Decie, he had began to cast about in his mind for the spring which impelled the machinery.

"He is a most estimable young man," observed the Baronet, with the same unconscious patronage—"a most estimable young man, though Victor says no."

"Um! the prejudices of the young are not generally at fault," Decie mused; "they act on impulse instead of calculation. I must get the immaculate Speedwell to grace my show by his presence; and," he concluded to himself, "it seems to me a little mesmerism will be beneficial to all parties."

IX - LIGHT AND DARKNESS

As the quiet years had stolen on there had come but little change in the house where the Abrahams had their abiding place. Time passed, bringing all its petty cares and anxieties—to Abishai the money his soul coveted, for he had grown rich beyond his wildest dreams. The great strike had been followed by a spell of prosperity and, naturally, speculation. The hunchback had the genius of money-making. Waste lands, at one time scarcely worth the few mountain sheep which grazed the scant herbage, was now transformed into stately wharves and prosperous streets. Little by little Abishai had invested in land, till at twenty-five he found himself master of a fortune. It had been a golden time. Men had been only too eager to borrow money, reckless of the percentage they paid. Abishai laid himself out as a private banker. Pressure followed in due course. Over-production and over-trading is a tale which needs no telling. Abishai Abraham became rich.

Hazael had found his way into Armstrong's bank, and, content with his lot, had secretly married heedless of the future. Speedwell, who still lived in his old quarters, hinted at promotion, and made much of the younger son, for between him and Miriam there existed a strong attachment, and Philip Speedwell loved the girl with his whole heart and soul.

And well he might; for, in all his dreams of fair women, he had never seen aught like she. Miriam had grown into a beautiful woman, with all the grace and suppleness of her race. Her dark eyes, swimming and liquid, looked fire and passion; her face was clear and calm, with the nobility of feature and grand expression of an ancient priestess. And so thought Speedwell, as he stood watching her a few mornings later. Many a time had the declaration of his passion trembled on his lips; but, with all his audacity, he was afraid. One ray of light in the dark place fell fluttering upon the contour of her head. Speedwell flushed and trembled as he turned to her.

"Miriam," said he, "do you know how beautiful you are?"

She did not notice the tremor of passion in his voice, as she turned her glorious eyes upon him, with a glance half scornful, half amused, tolerating him as a fair young queen might tolerate a courtier.

"And if I do not, surely that is no fault of yours, Philip," she answered. "Even flattery grows distasteful by repetition; and I hate flattery."

"I almost believe you do; I almost think you have no heart at all."

"Ah! you think so," Miriam answered, dreamily. There was a tender, wistful smile upon her face which inspired Speedwell with vague alarm. "You think so. And what right have you to think that, Philip?"

"None at all," said he, moodily. "Would that I had. Nay, hear me out. When I came here I was poor and starving, and you were kind to me. I have never forgotten that. Now I am upon the high road to fortune; but I lack one thing I would have more than all the world."

A genuine emotion trembled in his voice—an emotion from his very soul, untainted by any leaven of worldliness or self. There was nothing cold, or calculating, or forced in his passion, as at times the worst of us is warmed by some pure and generous impulse. But Miriam, looking into his pale face and glowing eyes, read nothing of his thoughts.

"And what is that?" she asked.

He came forward, and laid a cold hand upon her warm, glowing arm.

"Cannot you guess?" he asked. "Is my devotion so well disguised? Surely you must know that it is your love I want. How I have worked for it, hoped for it! I would have waited a little longer, but I cannot. Turn your face to me."

"I am sorry," said Miriam, when the first shock had passed away—"more sorry than I can tell. Believe me I never expected this."

"Though it has been plain enough to all the house besides."

"I, at least, knew nothing of it. How should I? If you care for yourself and me, you will say no more, Philip. Let us spare each other unnecessary pain."

She turned towards him with a pitying smile. But he was not the man to yield the prize without a struggle, and her look sufficed to arouse all that was wild and reckless in his nature.

"What do I care for myself?" he cried. "You shall not play with me like this. I will have an answer, if I stay here all day."

"You shall!" she said, curtly. "We are not rehearsing a love scene now. I do not love you; I never shall. You should know my nature by this time. Come! let us be friends again," she continued, holding out her hand. "We must not quarrel. I am sorry for you, Philip, but no words of yours can alter my resolution."

There was a pleading look in her eyes that most men would have found it hard to meet. But Speedwell turned aside, ignoring the proffered hand, and wild with baffled rage and disappointment.

"I am unfortunate," he said, bitterly; "doubly unfortunate in not being the first in the field. So, as they say on the stage, I have a rival."

The hot Eastern blood began to boil and fret in the girl's veins. The rich colour mantled her cheeks, but she did not speak. Standing now with a steely glitter in her eyes which held no warning to the rejected lover.

"So this comes of these chance—if they are chance—meetings on the shore.

You aim high, Miss Abraham. I congratulate you upon your lofty ambition. Small wonder that I have no chance with the heir of Sir Percival Decie."

"You have been spying," Miriam cried.

She stopped abruptly, conscious of the depth of her admission. For she knew now, for the first time, how much she had valued these few chance meetings and pleasant words with Victor Decie, and how she had treasured up their recollection in her heart.

"You are convicted out of your own mouth," Speedwell pursued, unconscious of the whirlwind of passion he had aroused. "My suspicions——"

"Your suspicions!" cried Miriam, with flashing eyes. "And what right have you to suspicions? Play the spy on others, and leave me to myself. I was willing to spare you a useless degradation; now you force it upon yourself. I despise you! Go, and do you worst!"

Speedwell bowed to hide the wildness in his face.

"This is a defiance, then. Now I know the weak spot in your armour, and what to do. But this dainty young aristocrat, who injures me by his passing fancies, shall suffer yet. You little know the power I hold in my hands, Yes," he hissed, "you little know that I hold Sir Percival Decie's fortune in the hollow of my hand. When I strike the blow, we shall see if you can save your lover then."

"Yes we shall see," said Miriam, dreamily, then, in a wild burst of passion. "Go, If you do not want me to strike you! Go!"

She pointed, with scornful finger, to the door. He crept out smiling, though his face was set and white. Miriam watched him till he had gone; then a sudden trembling smote her in every limb.

The recollection of the past, the memory of a few pleasant words, an idle compliment or two, and she had lost her heart. And yet she was not sorry or ashamed, knowing full well that the realization of this simple idyll could never be. She had given her heart in all the abandonment of her passionate nature, unasked, unsought.

And now, for the first time, she understood what she had done. She did not sit down and weep, as we are told she should, for there was no sense of shame. Again was it possible that Speedwell's threat was true, and, if so, what could she do to avert the catastrophe which threatened? There was a vague feeling of mistrust in the air—a presentiment of coming evil. In the midst of this reverie, Hazael entered, his usually cheery face doleful and uneasy.

"I am troubled in my mind," said Miriam, in answer to his query. "I feel miserable."

"Do you? Well, so do I," Hazael answered, with a cheerfulness which belied his words; "and I want you to help me. But how to begin I don't know."

"Begin in the middle; it saves a lot of time.

"Perhaps I had better. Promise you won't scream. Miriam, I am married!"

"Yes," said Miriam, quietly. "I am not surprised. Go on."

"That is something off my mind, then," Hazael continued, with a visible relief. "I should have told you before, only I lacked the courage to do so. It was some months ago, now. The chief reason we kept it quiet was because of my position at the bank. Can you guess who it is?"

"There is no reason to guess, for I know. It is Aurora Meyer."

"How did you find out?" Hazael cried, in wild surprise. "You don't mean to say anyone knows besides ourselves?"

"It is a serious thing, Hazael, more serious than you suppose," said Miriam, reflectively. "Why did you not confide in me, or have a little patience? I am sorry for you, but how much more pity do I feel for your wife. You know the Meyers; you know how they would thrust her out of doors without hesitation if they knew. And this concealment cannot last."

"I was coming to that," said Hazael, ruefully. "There my schemes were all at fault, for you see there is something coming which makes any further concealment absolutely impossible."

Miriam's face became grave and her eyes thoughtful. She would have done anything, even unto death, to save this favourite brother from harm, but the present difficulty was far beyond her fragile diplomacy.

"Hazael," she asked, with a sudden ray of hope, "have you any money?"

He shook his head dolefully. As the degenerate creature of the family, he seldom had much at command, and the demand was unexpected.

"It is not immediately required, of course, but I have a plan, if the worst comes to the worst. But before doing anything further I must see her."

"I thought you would," Hazael replied, gratefully, "and, fortunately that can easily be managed. You know the old door at the top of the stairs?"

"It would be unwise to open that, after all these years."

"Perhaps; if it had not been opened before. But you will find it easy enough. I think that was managed very cunningly. However, I have arranged everything. Take this key, and do not be afraid, for the lock and hinges have been so well oiled that there is not the slightest sound. I promised Aurora you should be with her at twelve to-night. You are not afraid?"

"No, I am not afraid," Miriam answered. "And now leave me. Oh, Hazael! why could you not have told me or had a little patience?"

It was the only reproach she uttered, and yet she was contemplating one of the most heroic deeds of self-sacrifice.

The long day dragged on, bringing evening in its train. Supper time came, and they sat down. Rebecca quiet and calm, watching her convict husband as he ate his food in a savage sullen way, and saying nothing according to his wont. Abishai had placed a little book before him which he seemed to be studying carefully, almost lost to his surroundings. Speedwell sulkily quiet, with an evil gleam in his eyes. To Miriam the quiet was oppressive, every sudden sound made her heart beat faster. Presently one by one they slunk away, leaving the girl and Hazael alone. Quietly he left the room, and returned with the remark that they had all gone at last. Overhead here and there there was a sound of footsteps, and occasionally the fall of a boot; then silence.

Gradually time slipped on, till a church clock near at hand struck twelve with measured throbs. The two watchers looked quietly at each other, and without a word Miriam rose and walked stealthily upstairs. There was a creaking groan or two sounding in the stillness, like the crack of a pistol shot, but nothing more. With trembling hands she turned the key in the lock, and swung back the door. Then swiftly was it closed again, for a figure stood inside waiting like a ghostly shadow.

"Is that you?" Miriam whispered. "Is that you, Aurora?"

There was a sound like a murmur of acquiescence, then a pair of arms were thrown round Miriam's neck, and a head lay sobbing gently on her shoulder.

X – OVERHEARD

The gloom deepened till the distant spires and pinnacles faded into one black cavernous darkness, as if the whole world had been passed into solid penumbra; a perfect adumbration. Then lighter, till a pink gash broke the veil, and edged things lofty with a dim, luminous brightness, and still Miriam lingered. Day was not far off when the door opened, and she stepped back into a shaft of light thrown from an open door, full upon her face, which glowed with a certain softness and a holiness of purpose in her eyes. Swiftly she turned aside, for the door of Abishai's room was open. She caught one passing glimpse of the cripple seated, his chin resting upon his crutch, as he regarded intently the flushed countenance of Speedwell opposite. On a table between them lay plans and papers. Miriam would have passed on, but a name hissed through Abishai's tooth fell upon her ear. Then she hesitated, and listened.

"It is a pretty plan," said Abishai, in his harsh, croaking voice—"a very pretty plan. But will it work, think you? Victor Decie is no fool. If either of us offer to buy that waste land by the Old Meadow Works he will suspect."

"But we shall not buy it. Now let me make you a present of a pretty scheme, after your own heart. You know I am manager of Armstrong's bank—I am virtually the responsible head. Decie owes us over ten thousand pounds upon his current account. Now supposing I send him a letter in the morning, expressing regret that my directors are unable to see their way to honour any further drafts until some security is given?"

Miriam crept a little closer, her whole fibre trembling with excited expectation. Living all her lifetime in a house where business talk was the very air she breathed, she had no difficulty in following the technical discussion of the two knaves.

"Feasible," returned Abishai. "But I don't see how that is going to help us. In the first place, you could not refuse a deposit of deeds as security; and as Old Meadow is a new toy, they would be forthcoming fast enough."

"Oh, no! And I will tell you why. With the exception of The Moat and the home farms, we have Sir Percival's title deeds in our custody—not as security, mind you, but in charge for his mortgagees. You owe me something for the information I am always giving you, Abishai. And now what do you think of my plan for pulling up the haughty baronet?"

Abishai tapped his crutch upon the floor, his eyes gleaming. Miriam strained her ears to listen to his reply.

"You say you have the deeds of his property besides The Moat estate. Very good. Then, with what he is losing at Old Meadow, he can have very little capital at command. Now, suppose you not only stop his advances, but call upon him to pay the balance against him! He will come to you in a great rage, and you must quiet him down, as you can do, for you are an oily scoundrel, Philip, I will say that."

Speedwell laughed at this dubious compliment, and Abishai, tickled with the sense of his own grim humour, laughed in his turn. Presently the cripple continued his ruminations.

"He will bluster, no doubt; but he must have money, and moreover he must have it speedily. Then you will tell him where it can be found."

"Certainly," said Speedwell, with a curdling laugh. "I am so deeply attached to the family that I shall be pleased to help him. Only you see I don't know where to advise him to go."

"I am coming to that. You may casually mention to him that there is a poor but honest Jew, who is willing to accommodate him to the extent of 20,000 upon the security of The Moat."

"And where is this anomaly—the poor but honest Jew?"

"I am. I will lend Sir Percival Decie this money at five per cent."

Speedwell shot a keen glance at his companion; but there was no sign of jesting there. Evidently Abishai was in deadly earnest. The thin lips were pressed tightly together; his eyes shone with greed and malice.

"It will cost me something, for I can make more of my money. But it will pay me in the long run. He will come to me, you see, he will come to me, and then I will make my own terms. I shall require a deposit of deeds, and an unregistered bill of sale."

"And what use is that as against creditors?"

"There will be no occasion to wait for that. No; that part of my scheme is my own. Once I get that Sir Percival is ruined——"

Here his voice sank so low that Miriam could not hear his words. Moreover, she was puzzled now. That some diabolical mischief was on foot she knew by the intensity of her brother's voice, but what she could not tell, for the allusion to the bill of sale had gone far beyond her depth. It was nearly morning, too, and the faint, gray shadows began to loom through the early mists.

Still she lingered, unwilling now to lose a single word.

"Buy the waste lands between the Old Meadow Works and the shore," came Speedwell's voice, with rising inflexion, as of one who concludes a sentence. "Delay is dangerous. If they only find what is there, no scheming of ours will ever get Sir Percival Decie into the net."

"There is where we are at fault again. Ah, it makes me mad to see them piling up that worthless iron there, while a fortune lies under their very noses. And any day may discover it. Speedwell, we are within an ace of being the two richest men in the town of Westport."

"You're shrewd enough as a rule; can't you devise a plan?"

"I have a plan, a certain one," answered the hunchback, morosely; "only, like other things, it is a matter of time. What drives me nearly frantic is the thought of what some accident may produce. Every time I see a man looking wild and excited, I expect to hear they have found——"

Here the high staccato tones fell, till they died away to a whisper.

"I don't see how this bill of sale business is going to help you," Speedwell put in again; "besides, you will have security enough without that."

"Always get as much security as you can," said the money lender, sententiously; "there are such things as foreclosures. But the scheme I have got into my head concerns neither you nor any other man; 'a poor thing but mine own,' as the poet says. And now go to bed."

Speedwell rose with a prodigious yawn; an exaggerated yawn which did not in the least deceive his companion. Miriam moved towards the stairs, but determined now to hear the last of this conspiracy.

"Then we perfectly understand each other about Decie's overdraft?"

"Perfectly. I have a meeting of my employers tomorrow; at least, a meeting of the proprietors, and anything I advise they will do. I have only to throw out a few vague hints, and they will take alarm directly. We will give him his fill, never fear. And now good night, or, rather, good morning, for—

"Night's candles are burnt out, and jocund day

Stands tiptoe on the misty mountain-tops.

Sweet dreams, fair youth, of gold and copper."

Miriam flew up the stairs upon winged feet. She closed the door of her room, and, drawing up the blind, stood watching the calm strife between night and morning. She was in no mood for sleep now. The events of the evening whirled in her brain—Hazael's secret and Abishai's dark scheme. She stood looking into the gray sky, gradually brightening with the promise of the coming sun to opal, and saffron, and gleaming orange, with long streaks of flame-hued phantasy. Prosaic objects were fringed with gold, and damascened here and there where the gleaming light caught them. Then a bright gladness shot up in the eastern sky; a bird somewhere began to pipe, and on the pavement below a pair of clogs fell with noisy clack. Another, and another came, till a stream of feet passed by, with whistling, and singing, and the light laughter of women's voices. Miriam changed her dress and bathed her flushed face in water, which felt cool and soothing.

It was ten o'clock before she got away, and then she turned her steps towards the sea. The dew still lingered on the hedges in crystal jewellery; the scent of dog roses filled the air with a subtle fragrance. Presently the living ocean lay before her, but she turned aside, walking across the wide sands to a spot where tall chimneys rose and a pall of hazy smoke drifted inland. The stillness became broken by the din of hammers and the war of machinery. Perspiring men dragged glowing globes of metal after them, to be dexterously cast upon an anvil, and be crushed and beaten into rails and bars. In the outer yard stood the object of her search, standing with a plan in his hand, talking to a tall, spare man, with clean-shaven face and twinkling eyes. Then for the first time she blushed and hesitated, scarce knowing what to say, and conscious of the difficult task before her.

The stranger turned, and stood struck by the beauty of the girl. Victor Decie came forward, with a bow and a smile, with that easy manner and pure, unaffected pleasantness which had won him so many friends.

"This is a pleasure, Miss Abraham," he said. "You wish to see me?"

Miriam trembled at the sound of his voice, knowing the deep joy she felt in his presence. She checked the feeling sternly.

"It is business, not pleasure," she said, icily, meanwhile, womanlike, chiding herself for her very coldness. "I would speak to you for a few moments alone."

The stranger bowed, and turned away, walking almost to the marge of the sea. With his eyes resting upon the ground, as if searching for something diligently, he straightway forgot the others.

"I am always at your disposal," said Victor. "Tell me what I can do for you."

"Mr. Decie, perhaps I am doing wrong," Miriam returned; "but, believe me, I am actuated by your welfare. Tell me the whole truth. Are you losing money in this place?"

"If you put it like that, we are. But it seems strange that——"

"Yes, yes; I know. And it takes much capital, more ready money than you have at hand to keep things going. You will be hard pressed for money shortly, and have to seek it elsewhere. Promise me that when it is offered, you will decline to accept it from that quarter."

Miriam stumbled on, blushing and trembling, partly from shame, partly from the feeling of her own helplessness, and knowing how badly she was stating her case. Victor Decie looked grave—almost displeased.

"If you do not mind being a little more diffuse," he said, coldly, "perhaps I shall be able to follow your meaning better."

"Oh! I cannot, I cannot tell you more. But you shall promise me one thing.

Believe me, I know much; perhaps, more than you. Promise me if you value your own happiness that this money I mention shall not come through the hands of my brother."

Without betraying Speedwell's perfidy, she told him all she knew. Victor listened gravely. Then he held out his hand.

"I cannot—see it yet," he said; "but I can see you have tried to do me a great service, and I thank you. It shall be as you wish. And now, if it is in my power, how shall I repay you?"

"Easily," said Miriam, in a tow voice. "I know you will despise me; but will you—will you lend me ten pounds?"

Victor quietly handed over a note, saying nothing. Miriam took it with trembling fingers.

"You must despise me," she said, brokenly; "but some day you shall know. You have amply repaid me now. And one thing before I go. Remember that, whatever misfortune happens—and they will happen with the most prosperous —you must not let Sir Percival dream of giving anyone a bill of sale."

XI - 2,458,160

As the case usually happens, when we have done something to be ashamed of, Miriam gave herself far more worry and anxiety over the all-important ten-pound note than the donor, by far. Victor Decie never doubted that it was required for some good purpose; and, being young and, consequently, a lover of beauty, pondered upon it for a moment, and straightaway forgot all about it. Miriam carried the note home, with hot cheeks and downcast eyes. On the earliest opportunity, she handed it over to Hazael for safe custody, in pursuance of the plan she had laid; and the latter, in his turn, thinking gold more available than notes, placed it in the shop cashbox, taking out ten pounds, and leaving the note in their place. It is certain that Victor Decie had forgotten the incident, for a month went by without Miriam's warning being in any way conformed.

Meanwhile, to use a conventional expression, the Professor had not been altogether idle. It suited his easy-going Bohemian nature to remain at his old lodgings, making friends of the frequenters of the house—mostly miners, these latter—and livening the monotony by records of his adventures and the occasional introduction of some smart trick with cards or, indeed, anything which came handy. It had been easy enough for him to scrape acquaintance with his nephew, especially as he had a more than passing knowledge of mineralogy, though Sir Percival shook his head over this, and groaned when he heard of his son's occasional visits to the Blue Dragon.

But by this time the electro-biologist's exchequer had reached a low ebb; and, to quote a pet phrase of his own, he had now nothing left besides a little honour, more audacity, and a most perfect acquaintance with the occult sciences. He had found not only a hall suitable for his lectures, but also a confiding printer of a sanguine and enthusiastic temperament, who had agreed to do the necessary bills upon the mutual system. Accordingly, a night was chosen; great names figured upon the posters; and, in fact, everything was prepared, and the only thing wanting was a little cash to meet current expenses. But even here the man of resources was not to be beaten. In his pocket he carried a property watch, as the dramatists' say, not that it was property in the sense that it was not 'what it seemed'; in fact, it was more, being a handsome gold watch, having a double case and an inscription to the effect that it had been presented to Signor Sartori by his grateful patron, Alexander Czar of All the Russias, in acknowledgment of unique and extraordinary talent. Among audiences in small towns this was no small attraction when handed round carelessly during the 'faking' part of some conjuring trick; also was it useful on occasions when the Czar's friend became short of ready money.

The eminent mesmerist, having determined to place the treasure in safe keeping for a time, waited one evening till the friendly darkness cloaked his movements, and proceeded, more by chance than design, to Abraham's side door. A moment later he was standing in one of the little boxes peculiar to a pawnbroking establishment with the watch in his hand. It was a quiet night, with very little business doing. Hazael had nothing in connection with the shop, and Abishai was away. Miriam herself came forward.

For a moment the easy assurance of the man of the world left him. He stood struck by the majestic beauty of the girl, wondering, vaguely, if this could be the daughter of his old servant. Miriam held out her hand, Decie passed the watch across mechanically.

"You want an advance upon this?" she asked, in a business-like manner.

"Well, yes. Unfortunately I am compelled temporarily to part with this treasure. 'Sweet,' says the poet, 'are the uses of adversity.' How much?"

Miriam could not repress a smile at this characteristic pathos as she turned away to examine the watch more closely. With a dexterity born of long practice she opened the case, and taking a little phial from a shelf poured a drop of acid upon the metal.

"It is very valuable," she said at length. "Anything up to twenty pounds."

"Which is twice the amount of my modest needs. Let us say ten."

"Very good." She went through a rapid calculation. "If you will give me ten shillings I will give you a note, if that is convenient. And the name——?"

"Is, as you see, Signor Sartori, of world-wide renown. There is the ten shillings, which I may say, by the way, is somewhat exorbitant. But it is not in my nature to haggle with beauty over coppers. 'Filius argentum est amo, vortatibus amum.' As soon would Anthony have made an inventory of

Cleopatra's pearls. I thank you."

So saying, Trevor Decie placed the note and little yellow ticket in his pocket, and, seeing no further opening either for conversation or compliment, made his fair attendant an impressive bow and left the shop.

He felt a singular sense of elation in the possession of money, a feeling which had for some time been strange to him. Under a lamp he took the crisp, clean note from his pocket again, and gazed on it affectionately, noting the number, 2,458,160, and remembering the combination of figures. Then he turned his steps in the direction of the Blue Dragon.

There was more than one attraction there. Firstly, the touch of old times in the dog-like fidelity of Saul Abraham; and, secondly, Speedwell was by no means an unfrequent visitor in the bar. Decie had begun to study the young man's character, nor did his investigations tend to improve his opinion of his son. He had set him down in his mind as crafty and unscrupulous. When he entered the little lighted room some time later they were both there.

Abraham greeted the new-comer with a respectful demeanour; Speedwell with an unpleasant smile. He was not exactly afraid of the Professor, but he had an uneasy consciousness that the latter had found him.

"Have you found many victims here?" Speedwell asked, with peculiar insolence. "Is the show likely to be a success, Signor Sartori?"

"Will you come and see?" returned the Professor, cheerfully. "I am certain of most of the nobility and gentry; you had better be present to represent commerce—honest and honourable commerce."

"If it will be any charity to you, of course I will come. You can put me down two nights for a front seat. Perhaps it would be a convenience to you to have the money now?"

"Not at all, my dear sir—not at all. Poor as I am, I can trust you. See what it is to have a name for posterity. 'Virtus nec cripi nec surripi potest.' Would that I could say the same."

In this light and airy badinage, with its undercurrent of satire, the Professor's trite quotations, culled from the early recollections of a well-learnt Latin grammar, stood him in admirable stead. When a ready repartee failed him, he always had one at hand, and that they were incomprehensible to the victim made them none the less potent.

"You are fortunate," said Speedwell. "I have not had the advantage of a classical education."

"Ah, the chaplain was probably a Cambridge man!" the Professor interrupted, with a glance which made the other's face flame with the passion he dared not gratify. "Moreover, I am not quoting the classics."

"For a man of such varied attainments, you do not seem to have been successful," Speedwell commenced, scarcely knowing what he was saying. "It is a pity to see so talented an individual gaining a precarious living by gulling fools."

"Neat, almost epigrammatic, but, like most epigrams, wrong. The living is not so precarious, and fools are scarce, or you would be better off. Behold!"

With an exaggerated theatrical gesture, the professor laid his ten-pound note upon the table, and signified to Speedwell that he might gaze at the phenomenon.

He did so; coming nearer with an assumption of incredulity.

"I congratulate you," he said; "for up till now I thought——"

He stopped suddenly, and reeled back as if the innocent piece of paper had been some deadly reptile. His pale face was paler still, his lips white, but not with fear or fright, but with some strange emotion which even the professor, with his knowledge of men, failed to understand.

"Where did you get that?" he gasped. "Tell the truth, man—where?"

"You are agitated, my good friend, and, besides, your manner does not invite the gentle confidence. If you will explain yourself."

Speedwell controlled himself with an effort.

"I beg your pardon," he said, with an assumption of ease which did not deceive the other. "It is a little mistake that is all. I—I took your note for one which I lost under somewhat mysterious circumstances some time ago. I see I am wrong."

The professor, with a bow and a smile, changed the conversation, but made a note of what had transpired. He turned away from Speedwell, and began to discourse in a low voice with Abraham. Presently he left the room without displaying any further interest in a matter, and a few minutes later walked into the same department in the pawnbroker's shop again.

Knowing hardly why, it was his intention to find from whence the note had originally come. Miriam came forward again, and in answer to his query told him. It was the same note Victor Decie had given to her; she had no object in disguising that from her questioner. Why the money had passed was no business of his, and he did not ask. When he emerged from the shop there was a slight smile of triumph upon his lips.

It being an off-day on the morrow, he set out the following morning to follow up his clue. Victor Decie, he found, had actually paid over the note to Miriam; also that he had two more consecutive in number to the one which had had such a powerful effect upon Speedwell. They had come, he found, in payment of an account from a small iron merchant in Westport a few days previously. The professor took the numbers, and, after pledging his informant to say nothing upon the subject, turned his steps in the direction of the town, with the intention of calling upon the iron merchant forthwith.

But from the factor in iron he gleaned little information, save that the three notes had been paid to him by a furnishing ironmonger. And accordingly to the other tradesman Trevor Decie went.

He found him extremely busy, but courteous. He would look in his ledger, and did. Fortunately, he had the number of the notes, hoping a little nervously that there was nothing wrong. The amateur Lecocq hastened to reassure the politely fussy individual upon the subject of his fears.

"It is entirely a matter of accommodation," he said, fluently. "If you can tell me who paid you these notes I shall be obliged. But do not for a moment put yourself out."

But the shopkeeper insisted upon giving the information. After consulting an assistant, he came forward, wearing an air of bland triumph, as a man who has solved some difficult problem.

"Yes, sir; I can tell you where they came from. They were paid to me as the last instalment on some furniture. The customer is—let me see—Mr. Lord—Arthur Lord—a young man, a most estimable young man, in the post office here. His address is 28, Lower Weston-street. If you want to see him——"

But the Professor disclaimed any such intention. He thanked the volatile tradesman and left, walking home quietly, his hat drawn over his eyes in dreamy meditation.

"An estimable young man in the post office," he mused, "who has command of thirty pounds at a time—'um! And that expression upon the immaculate Speedwell's face—was it fear, or triumph, or emotion? A mixture of all three I should say; quite a comedy face, in fact. Mr. Arthur Lord's description is so inviting that I must make his acquaintance; and then—estimable young man in the post office—we will test the efficacy of electro-biology!"

XII - TURNING THE SCREW

All his life Sir Percival Decie had been a sanguine man. Everything needful had come to his hand naturally. Now his courage began to fail him. Still further fell the depression in the iron trade. He had heavy engagements to meet, and very little wherewith to meet them. True the title deeds of The Moat estate remained in his possession; but if those went, and certain large calls he dreaded were suddenly made, he would be face to face with bankruptcy.

And just at this moment Speedwell, knowing the Baronet's affairs better than he knew them himself, took the opportunity of forging his thunderbolt, and dropping it plump into the midst of all Sir Percival's delicately-laid schemes.

The letter the manager wrote on behalf of his employers was courteous and respectful to the last degree; but at the same time admitted of no misconstruction. He pointed out that the account was heavily overdrawn, without anything like adequate security, and Messrs. Armstrong were getting anxious. Perhaps Sir Percival would call upon him (Speedwell), and talk the matter over.

Accordingly he repaired to the bank, where he found Speedwell awaiting him.

There was some deference in the young manager's manner; but something of power also. Sir Percival quickly realized that he was in the presence of one who knew his strength, and, if needs be, meant to use it.

"I must say your letter came upon me as a great surprise," Sir Percival commenced. "To be frank with you, I do not quite see how I can comply with your request at the present moment. Of course I can give you security. A deposit of deeds, no doubt, will be all you require?"

"I am afraid not," Speedwell answered, with gentle melancholy. "My employers are not fond of that class of security, especially—pardon me if I speak plainly—your account is one upon which little business seems to be done."

"But you cannot refuse to listen to my offer. Besides, this is so sudden; indeed, I am almost justified in calling it shady practice."

Speedwell smiled deprecatingly.

"Scarcely that, Sir Percival. We can afford to have no sentiment in business. Besides, your overdraft is an unusually large one."

"And if I give you ample security, you will charge me something like ten per cent. upon it. Really I fail to see what better arrangement you can make."

"It is not legitimate banking, sir, which is the great drawback. Candidly, my employers are frightened. I—I hesitated to mention such a thing in my letter to you, but I have received the most peremptory instructions that unless a large reduction—say 5,000—is made by Wednesday, I am to place the matter in the hands of our solicitors."

Sir Percival gasped. The times must be out of joint when he, a Baronet of ancient lineage, could be so calmly threatened by an obscure bank manager; a clever, pushing nobody, who had literally climbed out of the mud to respectability. Still, the look of respectful deference was on Speedwell's face; the one spot of oil which soothed the outraged Decie pride and arrogance.

"You are a young firm, sir; a young firm, and in danger of being spoilt by success," he answered, loftily; "but no business carried out on those autocratic lines can possibly stand. Now, put the matter to yourself as a man of some astuteness, how can I possibly find this money by the day after to-morrow?"

Speedwell was drawing vague lines upon his blotting pad. The face was calm, almost sad, with subservient sympathy, but his heart was beating fast. He took time before he replied, as if meditating deeply upon this unanswerable question. When he spoke again it was slowly and deliberately.

"As to that, Sir Percival, a man like yourself, who has available security, can have no difficulty in finding money at any moment. Allow me to speak to you, if you will pardon the liberty, as a friend. It is not for me to say so, but I think my employers are dealing harshly with you; a fact I ventured to point out. If you could make this reduction promptly, I could show them that I was right, and, moreover, give you a sounder position."

"There is something in what you say," answered the Baronet, grimly, "only, unfortunately, it is impossible. In the meantime, I must draw upon you——"

"No, sir; there I am powerless to help you. Pending this reduction I am instructed to honour no drafts of yours."

Speedwell was pale now, but no whiter than the victim opposite, for this determination meant, in as many words, ruin. Sir Percival, utterly overcome, covered his face with his hands and groaned aloud.

"Then I am undone, indeed," he murmured. "This morning I sent away cheques for more than twelve hundred pounds. It is true they will not be returned to you until Wednesday, which gives me a little time. Mr. Speedwell, you are a shrewd man; tell me what I must do?"

Speedwell shook his head mournfully, looking with sympathetic eyes into Sir Percival's white, stricken face, saying nothing. Then he turned towards the door, which opened at this moment, and disclosed a face, followed by a crooked, mis-shapen body, dragged painfully forward by a crutch. Abishai Abraham limped in, all unconscious of the presence of a third person, till, catching sight of the Baronet, he made a motion of obeisance and retired. Speedwell followed him with his eyes; his face lighted.

"I will see you in a moment, Mr. Abraham, if you will kindly wait in the outer office," he cried; and, turning to Sir Percival, continued. "That is the very man you want. What wonderful luck that you should have come in this morning! Mr. Abraham can doubtless accommodate you to any amount you require. What do you say, sir?"

The vision of his cheques dishonoured floated before the Baronet's eyes. He had a holy horror of moneylenders and their ways, but it was a question of the sternest necessity. Moreover, he was human. What a triumph it would be to pay off the whole of his overdraft, and leave himself in credit! For a moment he hesitated, finally consenting to see the accommodating Jew.

Speedwell turned away, mistrusting the fierce joy glowing in his face.

"I think you have decided wisely," he said. "Allow me to present you with the use of my office till you have settled the preliminaries. And a word in your ear, Sir Percival; if you press for the money to-day, you may have it."

A moment later, Abishai Abraham crawled in, his face wreathed in a fawning smile, his thin lips prim and set in all humility. He seated himself upon the extreme edge of a chair, and sat meekly, as if he had come to seek some precious favour at the hands of his hereditary enemy.

"You wished to see me, Sir Percival?" he whispered. "If I can do anything in my poor way for so great a gentleman, command me. If it is money you want —and all gentlemen want money—I may help you."

He writhed about, rubbing his hands together, and smiling unpleasantly.

Sir Percival answered curtly, not relishing this poor pleasantry. "It is a large sum I want, Mr. Abraham. Your time, doubtless, is valuable; so is mine. In a word, I want twenty thousand pounds."

"A huge sum—a great sum. Ah, yes! And you want all that, good sir? And if I can find so much, what is the security?"

"The security will be a note of hand, accompanied by The Moat title deeds. You know the property and the rental it produces."

Abishai scraped his chin with his lean yellow claws, the colour of the gold he loved so well. He smiled to himself as he called to mind the time years ago when he had gathered from the floor the money Sir Percival had left with his mother.

"The beautiful Moat is well known—yes. Embracing the works, eh?"

"That will form no part of the security, of course," Sir Percival stammered. "There is a separate mortgage on that which, however, does not touch the freehold."

"Very good, Sir Percival. You will want this money at once. And you can have it this very afternoon if you wish it so."

He waited for this statement to strike the Baronet with its full force. Experience had taught him that the sight of the money, the promise of speedy fulfilment lured many a victim into the net, and he was not wrong now. Sir Percival coloured slightly, partly with relief, though the feeling of the retaliation he was about to bring on Armstrong and Co. was uppermost.

"But," paused Abishai, "there is one other little thing. I shall require you to assign to me the household furniture and effects of The Moat, I shall."

"But this means a bill of sale."

"No, Sir Percival, nothing of the kind, for it will not be registered. That is a matter of form I make it a rule to insist upon. There is nothing more to be said. If you consent to sign this harmless little document, you may make an appointment, and get the money this very day."

For one moment Sir Percival hesitated; then the recollection of his liabilities rushed upon him, and he was lost.

"I consent," he said, "strictly on the understanding that this is a mere matter of form. Fix your own hour and place, so long as it is before the bank closes, and I will meet you with the deeds."

"Then let it be at the Angel, at three. We can have a private room there, and settle the matter in a few moments. Does that please you, sir?"

Sir Percival intimated that it did. The Angel, moreover, was the principal hotel in Westport, a huge building with assembly rooms and accommodation for invitation balls and meetings. It was here that Professor Sartori had decided to give his entertainment. So in the afternoon, when Abishai and the Baronet met together upon the steps, the Professor was coming down. He made them no sign of recognition, but as they passed him he hesitated for a moment, and returned. It was the first night of his performance. Behind the stage were two rooms—dressing-rooms to be used during any entertainment—and shut off from the stage by sliding panels. Usually they were used as business apartments, as now, for it was market day in Westport, and the hotel was full. Into one of these the Baronet and his companion were shown, where a third individual awaited them, a solicitor and tool of Abraham. The Professor, having satisfied himself of their presence, disappeared into the great hall, and, creeping quietly upon the stage, laid his ear against the panel and listened.

The voices were quite distinct, save the third one, who was mumbling through some legal document. When he had finished Sir Percival spoke.

"I understand this is quite a matter of form? That is perfectly clear then. And I am to sign here? Certainly. Give me a pen."

There was a sound as of a pen scratching over some hard paper; the crisp crackle of some material which the listener concluded, and rightly, to be parchment. Then the third person spoke in a quick low voice; a murmur of acquiescence, and again another rustling, evidently the soft flutter of bank-notes.

"I think you will find them right, Sir Percival," said Abishai. "Two hundred hundreds. Perhaps you would like to count for yourself."

There came a confused murmur of voices, amidst the crackling of papers, and bank-notes, and parchment; the noise of something being stowed away, and then Sir Percival's bland, patronising accents as he wished his companions good afternoon. The listener lingered till he heard the sharp creak of the Baronet's boots echoing down the passages.

"You are sure this secures to me the waste lands round the Old Meadow Works?" came Abishai's low rasping tones. "There is no mistake about that."

"No, indeed, Mr. Abraham, there is no mistake, sir."

"Very good. And directly the first instalment of interest is overdue I am in a position to levy execution upon the effects at The Moat."

Mumble, mumble came the stranger's voice in the quick low accents of one who strives to make his meaning clear. There was a hoarse, unpleasant laugh, followed by a low chuckle, and Speedwell's name was mentioned. A minute later Abishai walked down the steps of the Angel into the street with a gleam of unholy joy in his face; but the listener behind the panel smiled too, and his smile was more deadly dangerous than that of the successful Jew.

XIII – MAGIC

A month had passed away. Leafy June had melted into the languid embrace of her twin sister, and rudely August was at hand. There had not been much change, save that Sir Percival had taken a dignified revenge upon Armstrong and Company, and the Professor's show had been a genuine success.

The great hall was a blaze of light, and Westport's chivalry had gathered there. The magnates of the busy town arrayed in solemn rows to witness the performance which had made such a stir in the place. Sir Percival and his son, the former, protesting against all such trickery and humbug, yet curious withal, were seated side by side with Mark Lockwood and his daughter, and next to them Philip Speedwell, a smile of incredulity on his face, and a hope in his heart that Signor Sartori might speedily be confounded.

"There is nothing creepy about the preparations," Ida Lockwood remarked to Victor, indicating the bare stage, containing only a plain deal table and a few chairs. "It is not my idea of a wizard's cave."

"The fellow is very clever, though," replied Victor; "I wouldn't have credited it if I hadn't seen for myself."

"Clever from a histrionic point of view," Speedwell sneered. "The confederates, I must say, are well drilled. But surely, with your astuteness, Mr. Decie, you don't believe this strength of will business is true?"

"I am weak enough to think so—yes. Perhaps in the interest of the audience, and for your own satisfaction, you had better test it. I have."

"And found it powerless, no doubt," Speedwell spoke sarcastically. "The medium was not sufficiently charged with the magnetic current, or you were not a receptive subject; failure glibly accounted for by choice phrases, eh?"

Victor smiled grimly.

"My experience was not precisely that; I am a firm believer. If you can prove the Professor a charlatan, perhaps you will do so."

"That is a challenge," Speedwell bent forward and whispered, "and I accept it. I will bet you a five-pound note I not only go upon the stage, but also that I come away again in my right mind. Come."

"Done," Victor returned, curtly, as he turned away.

Speedwell was no favourite of his, and he felt annoyed now that he should have been betrayed into making such a wager. Miss Lockwood laid her hand upon his arm and indicated the stage, where the Professor was standing now, bowing right and left. His eyes were keen and piercing, as they roamed about the large room, as if searching for someone; then he seated himself upon a chair with folded arms. Presently an attendant brought in a large blackboard and placed it upon trestles in the centre of the stage. Upon this the Professor traced in chalk the figures:—

Every eye was turned upon the board in silent expectation. Then, as if this had nothing to do with the entertainment, the performer turned to the spectators again. Would one of those present come upon the stage? There was the usual hush of expectation. Speedwell made a motion as if to move, then changed his mind, determining to wait and confound the Professor in his hour of triumph. At length a sound of feet was heard in the background, and, with an assumption of ease, a youth came forward and walked, blushing at his own temerity, on to the stage.

"I am obliged to you," said Sartori, with a bow. "I promise that you shall be restored to your anxious friends unhurt. Take a seat, and amuse yourself with to-day's paper." All this time the speaker had his keen eyes fixed upon his victim, who had already began to follow him with a dazed fascination. "Come, take up the paper. You are not afraid?"

"N—no," the youth stammered; "I ain't afraid; but I can't pick it up."

"Can't pick it up? Dear me! some of these papers are remarkably heavy. Now, attend to me. See this sovereign which I place upon the floor. Now, if you can pick it up, it is yours. Try."

With great eagerness the victim, on hands and knees, grasped at the coin, but to him it was immovable, as if it had been screwed to the floor. The Professor bade him rise and return to his chair.

"Do you feel very tired?" he asked.

"No—yes. I am tired. I can't keep my eyes open."

"Then go to sleep." And in a few moments the lad lay back in his chair, his head upon his breast, fast asleep.

There was a little murmur of applause, some astonishment, but, as yet, cynical silence from the front seats. They had most of them read about these things, and, as yet, refused to be convinced. Speedwell smiled incredulously at the specious humbug, and patiently waited for his turn to come.

The hall became a little darker as the lights turned down; the mystic figures on the blackboard began to glow with an incandescent brightness, gradually taking the form of a luminous bank note, roughly sketched, but unmistakably the representation of a 10 note. Suddenly the gas flared up again, and it was gone, leaving only the chalk figures behind.

The Professor looked keenly at his audience, and noted the ghastly pallor of Speedwell's face as he met his eyes. But a few rows behind was another face, white and chill, the third actor in the little drama of which Sartori was the prompter.

"I want another gentleman," he said. Who will come?"

A desperate courage fired Speedwell's heart. He stepped forward on to the platform, and stood facing the Professor, who welcomed him with a smile as he looked him in the face, speaking smoothly and rapidly.

"I am obliged to you, though I am afraid you came here in no friendly spirit. You think this is all trickery; but you shall see. I am pleased to welcome a gentleman so well known and respected; a Philistine, whose conversion will be to my credit. You are listening?"

Speedwell had been listening to the words, which, clear at first, now began to sound drowsily in his ears, like distant water. He was conscious of a certain vague terror, a wild yearning to get away, but the glittering eyes seemed to chain him to the spot. A drowsy languor stole over his senses, a feeling of peace and quietude, as he sank into a chair with a contented sigh.

Sartori turned to his first victim, and, touching him gently, whispered something in his ear. He rose with eyes wide open, though with no gleam of consciousness in them, and, stepping from the stage, felt with his hands till he came to the fourth row of reserved seats. There he hesitated for a moment, then, passing down between the people, walked along till he came to the object of his search—a young man, who hung back with every appearance of lively fear. But the sleeper would not be denied. Surely but gradually he drew the spectator from his seat amidst shouts of unconstrained merriment, and bore him unwillingly towards the stage.

There were beads of perspiration on his face which was white with terror. Sartori noticed that the hand he took hold of to help this third victim up was cold and clammy. But he was playing now a drama which was not on the bills, and caviare to the general.

"You may go," he said, turning to the original victim. "I shall want you no longer. Ah, you fancy you are asleep! Bless me! you are no more asleep than I am. Go back to your seat again."

The lad rubbed his eyes and looked round in surprise. Then, with a hasty glance at his tormentor, he fled. Sartori turned to the new comer. He was absolutely shaking with fear, a terror which the spectators mistook, and roared again.

"Spare me—oh, spare me!" shrieked the miserable man. "I am young. I have done no harm to you. Let me go!"

The audience screamed with laughter. This lively fear was a treat they had not expected, a part of the performance they could not understand. Sartori, with his eyes fixed upon the fearful one, made a few quick passes with his hand, and gradually the cries subsided to a gurgling sob. Then the Professor came forward with a low bow, and seemed as if he would speak. He was very pale, and began in a low voice expressing his regret that the performance could not continue. There was an old proverb, he said, to the effect that the sword will in time wear out the scabbard. He had been through two arduous performances that day, one of which had been extremely trying. Nothing but consideration for the feeling of his patrons had enabled him to carry on so long. He (the speaker) staggered slightly. He would throw himself upon their clemency.

Whereupon the band struck up the National Anthem, and amidst confused murmurs and expressions of forcible disapproval from the background, the curtain came down, and the audience filed out. Scarcely had the last of them disappeared when the door was locked. Sartori recovered himself marvellously.

There was no sound save the laboured breathing of Speedwell and his companion in misfortune. He roused the latter roughly, indicating at the same time the mystic figures upon the blackboard.

"That is one of them," he said. "Only one! How many more were there?"

"I must think. I cannot tell you yet. My head is so confused." The words came slowly, painfully, as if forced from him. "I think a hundred altogether—yes, a hundred tens. They were posted here in a registered letter, and I took them. Don't ask me any more. You know too much already."

"A hundred tens you say," continued Sartori, calmly ignoring this appeal; "and you stole them as they passed through your hands? Ah, we are getting on! Was there no inquiry made for them—no reward offered."

"No, the sender dared not. He was bound to take his loss in silence."

"Delightful mystery. A man loses a thousand pounds, and takes the loss as a matter of course because he dare not make inquiries. This becomes interesting. There was a letter with this packet, of course?"

"Yes, a registered letter, addressed to—to 'Lock and Co., Greyfriars, London.'"

"Very good. And the contents of this wonderful epistle? I want to hear what it contained, to prevent the owner claiming the stolen property."

There was a long silence, as if the victim was striving with himself to shake off the influence which lay upon him. But the magnetic power was too strong to be so lightly thrown aside.

"Because," came the startling answer, "in the first place, these very notes had been stolen by the sender."

"I congratulate you upon your astuteness. No wonder you ran the risk of appropriating them. And the name of this honest gentleman?"

"Messrs. Armstrong's manager—Mr. Philip Speedwell."

The answer came with such swift surprise that the Professor was startled for a moment. That Speedwell's name should be mentioned was no matter for any great astonishment; but that he should have been so blindly reckless was a thing for speculation. For a time Sartori's nimble brain worked silently.

"Ah, so that is your safeguard! I need not ask if you have preserved this letter. If so, I must ask you to hand it over to me."

"Of course I kept it; but not here. Oh, no; it is not here. I—I have hidden it carefully. But not here. Oh, no; not here!"

"Come, hand it over!" retorted the mesmerist, coolly, "or must I take it by force? Don't trouble to look in all your pockets, when you know very well exactly where to put your hand upon it. Thank you."

The wretched Post Office clerk produced the letter and passed it over. Sartori gave it a brief glance, sufficient to see that Speedwell's signature was at the foot, marvelling, meanwhile, that so deep an individual was insane enough to put his name to a document so doubly criminating. He had all the information now he required. Then, with a few words, he brought back his informant to his senses.

"I—I. You have mesmerized me," he gasped, his eyes upon the fatal figures. "What did I say? What have I done?"

"We will talk more of that to-morrow, my friend. Meanwhile, rest assured that any secret of yours lies entirely between you and I. With the exception of the unbeliever there we are alone, you perceive; but the key is in the door, and you can let yourself out. And a word in your ear. If you dare to change another bank-note or destroy what you have, you shall sleep in Westport Gaol to-morrow night, sure as your name is Lord. Good night."

Lord reeled down the hall and out into the cool night air like a drunken man.

Sartori watched him till the door closed with a clang, and then turned to Speedwell, who was sleeping still.

"Who is Lock and Co.?" he asked, when he had brought the other to drowsy consciousness.

"I, and Abishai Abraham, and another; we are Lock and Co. Hush! Someone will hear you. It would ruin me if it got known. Don't tell Armstrong."

"I won't," Sartori answered, sardonically. "It would be a pity. So the capital this enterprising firm work upon is drawn from Armstrong and Co. Estimable young man—model son! And you are my son, I suppose," he continued, speculatively, "though I must confess I do not yearn for your affection. Indeed, if I consulted my inclination, I should hit you over the head with my stick. However, a little more information first. The honest Abraham, Abishai of that ilk, is extremely anxious to get possession of the waste lands round the Old Meadow Works. Why is this?"

"Abishai is cunning," returned Speedwell, thickly. "Abishai knows. Only don't you tell Sir Percival; but there is copper there—copper ore enough to make us the richest men in Westport. And now we have got the place, we shall all be millionaires."

The professor whistled softly. He had discovered symptoms of the metal by the seashore, though even he was not certain yet. And now this pretty pair of scoundrels had come in between him and his schemes. He sat down and contemplated Speedwell's drowsy features darkly.

Twelve o'clock struck—one, two, and three before Speedwell emerged from the hall, with unsteady footsteps and pale, perspiring face. As he walked home with the first blush of morning in the eastern sky, he began to wonder what he had said; or if he had betrayed any secrets of the prison house in his talk. For the first time in his life he was actually afraid of himself, and more afraid still of the sweet smile the Professor had bestowed upon him, accompanied by a benevolent good night blessing.

XIV - THE FIRST FRUITS OF SACRIFICE

Three weeks had Miriam been away, and yet she had made no sign to Hazel. Aurora was absent from Westport, too, and whether they were in communication or not the uneasy husband did not know. Yet Miriam had promised him that he should come through the coming ordeal unscathed, though as yet he had no conception of the sacrifice she was contemplating.

Things were still in this uncertain state when she wrote a single line, saying she was coming home.

It was evening when she arrived; a mellow August evening, with a warm glow in the air, and the drowsy hum of insects floating high. She had come from the station alone, and, as she walked into the little sitting-room where the late tea was laid out, she carried something in her arms which made Hazael's heart beat faster as he looked. Rebecca rose and came forward, as if to embrace her child; but there was something in the girl's look which held her back.

"Am I welcome?" asked Miriam. "Tell me that."

"Welcome enough, my child, but the question seems a strange one. Sorely have I missed thee. But what of our friends in Liverpool?"

"I know nothing of them, for I have not been there."

The strangeness of her manner arrested their attention. Miriam was pale, but calm; almost too calm, Hazael thought, as he shot her a swift glance. Yet she never turned in his direction.

"You have never been there!" Rebecca faltered. "And why? There is some strange mystery here. Sit down, child, and explain yourself."

"Presently. When I have spoken you shall judge of me again. Before I can be one of you again you must extend your welcome to this."

She bent forward, and with one hand drew back a veil from the burden she was bearing, and disclosed the features of a sleeping child. The picture she made standing in the background was a striking one. The mother's face was full of a nameless terror. Hazael moved forward as if to speak, but a swift, eloquent glance checked him. Abishai's eyes blazed, though he pressed his thin lips together, waiting. Speedwell pale as death, and raging inwardly in mingled jealousy and horrible fear.

"Perhaps you will be good enough to explain this comedy," he said, with a poor attempt at levity. "Miriam was always dramatic, but sometimes these appearances are open to misconstruction."

"There must be no misconstruction here," Miriam answered, calmly. "You shall judge for yourselves. The child is mine."

"No, no," cried Hazael, springing to his feet, "not you. You shall not say so! You shall not bring such disgrace upon yourself!"

"There is no question of disgrace for me. I—I speak the truth, and ask you for a welcome for me and mine. But the secret—and there is a secret—must, till the proper time comes, remain with me. Mother, can you trust me, when I say there is no shadow of disgrace in this."

"Rebecca had fallen forward on the table, covering her face in her hands; as yet she dared not trust herself to speak, for the fierce combat waging in her heart between love and duty—the stern duty of the Jewish creeds left her no thought or time for words. Then Abishai took up the parable.

"There is disgrace," he hissed, "gloss it over as you will. Put it to yourself, and tell me if it is not so. You will be peered at through the streets of Westport, mocked by every woman you meet, for none will believe such a tale. We have had dishonour enough without you adding to it. And this is all that comes of your beauty—to become a mark for scorn."

"Better be a mark for scorn, knowing in my heart that I have done no wrong, than like you!" Miriam burst out, passionately—"like you, hated and feared, as one who grinds the poor, and battens on their misfortunes; coining drops of blood into money; a miserable, despicable miser."

Her whole frame quivered with the violence of her emotion, so that she woke the sleeping child, who set up a pitiful wailing cry. The very sound sufficed to bring Miriam back to her womanly tenderness.

"Well, I am waiting," she continued. "Let me bear my sentence. Hazael, you will be on my side—come here." As he walked towards her, she whispered a few words in his ear, exhorting him to silence. "Speak, I am not afraid."

"You may stay for me," said Saul Abraham, breaking the awkward silence, and speaking low. "It isn't for me to judge you, my girl. You never threw my troubles in my face, and I don't forget it; but Abishai's master here, and what he says is law. And your mother's strict, too."

"If I am to be judged by letter of our creed then I am homeless indeed!" Miriam answered, mournfully; "but as you decide so shall it be. I will not stoop to defend myself again; the issue is in your hands!"

She had drawn herself to her full height, her eyes flashing, the moving, living embodiment of outraged innocence; but for the precious burden she held so tenderly to her heart. In spite of his belief Speedwell began to waver, but the demon jealousy was not so lightly to be tamed.

"Perhaps," he exclaimed, bitterly—"perhaps that declaration may be most satisfactory to another than I—Victor Decie!"

"What do you mean?" Hazael demanded, stepping forward. "Explain yourself, or, maybe, I shall force you to do so!" His threatening gesture was far more vehement than words. "What has Victor Decie to do with her?"

"What has he to do with her? Look there, and read for yourself."

He pointed to Miriam's face, dyed with a scarlet flame, her eyes bright and luminous, her mouth quivering. Rebecca let her hands fall upon the table again, and set up a mournful cry.

"Yes, I see it—I see it now!" she moaned. "And yet I have always prayed you to hate the name. And to come to this after longing all these years for the vengeance which has never come!"

"It is coming now; you will live to see that, mother," Abishai exclaimed. "A few weeks longer at the most, and then——"

He stopped with a long-drawn sigh. Miriam dashed the angry tears from her eyes, and turned to his contemptuous face.

"Ah, you think so—you think so! But it will never be, Abishai. All your deep-laid schemes will come to the ground; your cunning plot with Philip Speedwell there will not avail you."

"So you defend these hated Decies? Speedwell is right, then? Go to your lover, and ask him to shelter you? You have no home here!"

"And if you are right," she said, "am I not your own flesh and blood? You refuse me the hearing I should get from any stranger? To your hard heart, Abishai 'tis useless to appeal, I know! Mother, must I go?"

"Go, you must, for Heaven help me, is not my teaching stronger than my own mother's heart. Against us and your religion have you sinned! I dare not bid you stay! So, Miriam, you must go!"

Her head fell forward again, with groans and tears. When she looked up once more, Miriam had gone. She turned through the narrow shop out into the street mechanically, motioning that Hazael should follow her. For a moment he lingered, pouring out passionate reproaches, so that Miriam reached the street, where she stood in the still evening, alone. Almost unconscious of herself, she remained there waiting, till she noticed that Ruth Meyer was standing by her side, striving to attract her attention.

"Does it spread so quickly?" she asked, wearily. "Do you know already?"

The dark, elf-like creature nodded. There was a restless vivacity in her eyes, a curious twisting of the body, which bespoke a mind imperfect.

"I heard—yes. I was in the pawnbroker's shop, and through the ventilator I heard voices, and I listened. I am sorry, too—very sorry, Miriam, though we are not friends. Hazael stood up for you, though. Handsome Hazael! And I love him!"

"So you are sorry for me? Heaven knows, I need sympathy badly enough just now!"

"Miriam, my dear sister," Hazael had followed her out now. His eyes still glowed with the intensity of his late passion, though they grew misty now as he noted Miriam's dull, impassive despair. "I had not dreamed you would do this for me! Come back again, and let us speak! It is not too late yet! My whole soul revolts against such a sacrifice!"

"No, Hazael, I have chosen. My work must not be undone now; besides, I can bear it, and she cannot. I am made of sterner stuff than your——" She stopped, conscious of Ruth Meyer's inquisitive glance—"you know. And it will not be for long, Hazael. I have set my heart upon it."

Hazael would have answered warmly; all his chivalry was awake, his manhood aroused by the extent of this noble self-sacrifice. It seemed to strike him with fresh force, and yet he was powerless to help himself. Something must be done to relieve Miriam from the taint, but in so doing the blow would have fallen on another less able to bear its weight. Hazael would have answered warmly, when Abishai's voice arrested his words, He was standing in the doorway, pointing down the street with his crutch.

"Why don't you go?" he cried, working himself up to a pitch of frenzy. "Why don't you go; or will you stay there proclaiming your shame to the world?" He stepped forward, thrusting out his hand, "Go, I say! Bad enough it is, without seeking to make it worse."

Miriam shrank back.

"Abishai, would you strike me?"

"Ay, I would; and if you don't move, I will! Go!"

"A model brother, truly!" said a calm, even voice. Then a strong hand was laid upon Abishai's uplifted arm. "You would strike a woman, fellow? Your sister, too! Out upon you for a misshapen coward!"

Each of the short sentences was accompanied by a vigorous shake, and, finally, a hearty buffet, which sent the hunchback reeling back. The little group saw that Victor Decie was standing there, and by his side, a grim smile upon his face, and hands folded behind him, was Mark Lockwood.

"Nay, deal with him less harshly, Victor," said he, "for methinks thou hast the best of physical strength. Abishai Abraham, it is a sorry sight to see a strong man lay hand upon a woman. Why is this?"

"See the answer!" Miriam cried. She was herself again proud and contemptuous. "I bring this child home—mine, if you like, though its name is as pure as your own, sir; and because I cannot explain—because I will not say all I know, he, my brother, turns me out to starve!"

Lockwood's fine old face became singularly grave and sweet as he laid his hand upon the speaker's arm.

"Deception is wrong," he said; "but thy face has no trace of shame. I could almost think——"

"Sir! Can you be more merciful than my own flesh and blood? Can you look me in the face and see that I do not lie?"

"Peace!" the Quaker answered, sternly, seeing that Abishai was about to speak. Then for a long time he returned the girl's quiet, steady gaze. "Yea, I can see no trace of shame in thy features. I believe thee."

"Then, perhaps you will show her a little of the charity you boast of," the hunchback sneered, "for I promise you she shall have none here!"

"Abishai Abraham, thy counsel shall be followed. My poor lass, come with me, and thy wants shall be attended to, and oil poured into thy bleeding heart. I do believe thee to be pure and virtuous; and even if thou hast perchance deceived me, my duty must be done."

So, without another word, he beckoned for Miriam to follow him, and set out down the quiet street with the last rays of the sun falling upon his silver hair. Hazael caught the manufacturer's hand in a fervour of gratitude; Abishai leant against the lintel, like the shadow of a baffled sprite.

XV - A PLACE OF REFUGE

It was a quiet, peaceful homestead in which Miriam found herself. Castle-street, Westport, was a still thoroughfare, far enough from works and factories to enjoy restfulness and sunshine. Most of the houses had been built in the last century; large, solid-looking edifices, with long flights of steps and narrow windows; but behind each stretched large gardens and velvety lawns, showing the soft richness of a century. In one of these Mark Lockwood lived with his daughter, and hither he brought Miriam on that eventful night, and, with a few words of explanation, handed her over to Ida's care and keeping.

There was an unspeakable calm and restfulness about the place; an unspoken sympathy in the Quaker's daughter, which aroused all the gratitude and passionate gratefulness in Miriam's fiery, noble nature.

"I was a stranger to you, and yet you had pity upon me," she said; "whilst my own flesh and blood turned from me. You believe my sorry tale?"

"Yes," Ida replied; "I do believe you. I think you have made some great sacrifice to shield someone you love."

It was a fortnight later. They were seated in Miss Lockwood's own sitting-room, with the windows open and looking across the quiet lawn into the garden, resonant with the song of birds. Miriam stood with the fresh breeze blowing on her cheeks, where the hot colour burned and glowed with her emotion.

"Some day you will know—soon, I hope. Miss Lockwood, you have done me a great service; perhaps I shall be able to repay it. You do not know that my people are pledged to do one you love a lasting injury."

"I am afraid I do not understand. What harm have we done to yours, and so long as people are good and honourable, what evil can come to them?"

Miriam looked round the pretty room; all so bright and beautiful as refinement and wealth could make it. It seemed no part of the busy outside world, so far removed from care and anxiety as the Poles are asunder. What could its mistress know of the wickedness and depravity, the base passions and sordid sentiments of the outer hemisphere? It seemed to Miriam that no taint of worldliness had ever crept here, taking the light out of life, and robbing the warmth from the sunshine.

"You do not understand these things—how should you? You have never been brought in contact with everything that is mean and degrading. I have; and I have tried to raise myself above them. But it is hard work."

She spoke in short, broken sentences, her bosom heaving with a wild emotion.

"I have been brought up all my life to hate the Decies—we have all been taught that—but I cannot. And now there is a plot to ruin them—to ruin him, but not if I can help it."

Ida Lockwood listened in mild surprise; but gentle and unsuspecting as she was, there was something in the last words which grated upon her, a vague uncertain jealousy.

"You speak in language altogether beyond me," she said, coldly. "What is Mr. Victor Decie to you that you should speak of him like— like that?"

"What is he to me? What is the sun to the earth; the moonlight to the nightingale? I love him! Nay, hear me out. I know that he is pledged to you, that to him I am nothing, but I love him—ay, in a way you cannot understand. He has always had a pleasant word for me; a smile when others have met me with frowns; but who can explain those things? I love him!—I love him! I would give up my life for him, knowing that he would enshrine me in a tender remembrance. Why do I tell you this? I cannot say. It may be a shameful confession—nay, it is; but I never measured my standard by others. I have given my heart unasked, unsought; but I would not take it back if all the world lay at my feet!"

Miriam stopped at length, worn out by the violence of her passionate declaration. Her eyes were bright and shining, but there was a wistful, tender smile upon her face withal.

There was a long silence, broken only by the wild chatter of a starling perched upon a tree outside. Ida, a little shocked at first by the wild confession, began to feel a sense of deep pity for her companion. After all, perhaps, it was only natural that another might lose her heart to Victor.

"I am sorry, very sorry for you," she said, gently. "I wish you had not told me this, and yet there is no reason why we should be worse friends. Miriam, I cannot understand you."

"I cannot understand myself," Miriam answered, wearily. "I have been born too early or too late. I was never intended to be anyone's enemy but my own. But, mark me, there is some evil coming to those you love. To the best of my poor ability I have tried to ward it off, though I am fighting in the dark against those who would stick at nothing."

"But no harm can come to him," Ida exclaimed, with rising alarm. "He has not a single enemy in the world!"

Miriam laughed bitterly.

"Has he not? I know of two in my own family—my father and elder brother, Abishai. There is another more unscrupulous still, for he poses as a friend. I mean Philip Speedwell."

"Mr. Speedwell? Surely not. Consider what my father has done for him. He would not, could not, be so base as to strike a blow at us through Mr. Decie!"

"Did I not say you do not understand how far a man's wickedness can go. Philip Speedwell is a scoundrel. He has reasons for destroying Sir Percival Decie, of which I know nothing. He had reasons for injuring Victor Decie, because—I had better tell the truth at once—he thinks if he were out of the way I could bring myself in time to love him."

"Mr. Speedwell is your lover?"

"Mr. Speedwell thinks he loves me," Miriam corrected. "I hate him! I will not shock you by telling you his base suspicions, but I will tell you what I overheard one night at home."

Miriam's confession, trembling on her lips, was cut short at the critical point by the entrance of a servant, bearing the information that someone wished to speak to her. She walked into the morning-room, there to find Hazael pacing up and down, his face perturbed and evidently suffering under the influence of great mental distress. He was not so overcome that he forgot to embrace his sister tenderly and inquire after her welfare. Then he began to pace the room again.

"Hazael, you are in some trouble," Miriam exclaimed, "or you would not have come here. What is wrong now?"

"First, tell me about yourself. No reason to ask if you are happy here. I can see that. Are you beginning to repent your sacrifice, Miriam?"

"I shall never do that. Yes, I am happy enough. Now, let me hear what you have to say, for your face frightens me."

And, indeed, it might; for the features were white, and drawn, and haggard with something more than fear. Hazael paused in his stride, and, looking round, as if fearful that someone might overhear his words, fell into a chair, covering his face with his hands.

"I am beyond trouble almost, I am in despair," he said. "You know that I am in a respectable position at Armstrongs. Three days ago one of our customers left some negotiable securities with me—never mind what for, or what they were. We were just closing when they came in, so I locked them up in a drawer for the night. The next morning they were gone."

"What was the amount?" Miriam asked, at length.

"Three hundred pounds; it might just as well be three millions, for any chance I have of replacing the money. The suspense is driving me mad, and just now, as I was getting on so well."

He fell forward again, covering his face with his hands. Presently he resumed again.

"I have been wrong, I know, in not making the loss known at once, but I was afraid."

Crushed down as she was with her own troubles, Miriam could clearly see the seriousness of this new disaster. Not for a moment did she doubt the truth of Hazael's story. And yet there was small chance of his employers giving credence to this wild tale. At all hazards the money must be found, but how she had not the wildest conception.

"Hazael, I will help you if I can. Leave the matter in my hands, and I will speak to Mr. Lockwood. He will listen to what I have to say, and if you can be righted he will do so. Not but what I blame you for not speaking out at once. Go back to your business as if nothing had happened, and come to me this evening."

"God bless you, Miriam," Hazael said, brokenly. "You give me comfort, though I am afraid I am leaning on a broken reed. It is no easy task I am giving you, but I cannot face it myself."

"You will be righted, Hazael, and the real thief will be discovered, never fear. And now you must go, and trust me."

"I do trust you. Where should I be without your aid?"

So he went away, leaving Miriam to her painful reflections in the quietness of the room, where the noise of her heart seemed loud in the stillness, which was only broken by the mocking chatter of the starling, still perched upon the apple bough.

Hazael walked swiftly towards the busy streets seeing nothing, hearing nothing, but the wild whirl of his own painful thoughts. He had not got beyond the still thoroughfare when he met Aurora and Ruth Meyer. Sometimes he would have passed them, but now in his desperate mood, he stopped. Aurora's colour came and went; then, her own confusion past, she was struck by the whiteness of Hazael's face.

"Does the news concern us?" she cried, impulsively. "Is anything wrong with ____"

"Our family? No," Hazael answered, with a warning glance; "with me, much." And then, in his open, reckless manner, he told the listeners the tale he had poured into Miriam's startled ears.

It did not strike Aurora as strange that she should be standing there with Ruth by her side, listening intently. All discretion was swallowed up in her anxiety and devotion to the man she loved.

"I can tell you how to get the money!" Ruth cried, with a sagacious nod. "I can tell you, Hazael. Ah, yes."

Hazael and Aurora started guiltily; they had forgotten their companion.

"Indeed, Miss Ruth; I shall be obliged to you for the information."

"Abishai will lend it you—he has plenty. Only ask him."

Hazael smiled faintly in spite of his distress; the idea of Abishai lending the money struck him as being exquisitely absurd. He made some inconsequential reply, and then with a tender, significant glance at his wife, passed upon his way. Aurora and Ruth walked homeward, the latter, contrary to her wont, silent and meditative.

"Aurora, he must have this money."

"Of course," Aurora answered with an effort; "of course, and he will get it. But it is no affair of ours, remember; indeed, we should not have spoken to Mr. Abraham at all."

"But he shall have the money, handsome Hazael. And Abishai shall lend it him; crook-backed Abishai. I shall go and ask him, and if he refuses I shall kill him—kill him dead!"

So saying, Ruth made a wild pass with her hand as if striking down some imaginary foe. Her eyes gleamed with intentness of purpose, but Aurora saw nothing of this, for her whole vision was filled with the pallid whiteness of Hazael's despairing face.

XVI – REVENGE

Like a tiny snowflake, rolling downwards till it becomes a mighty avalanche, the news spread, gathering as it went, till all Westport knew that Armstrong's Bank had failed. It came to Mark Lockwood as he was seated in his office; it reached Ida and Miriam in their quiet seclusion. As it spread, the news came to Sir Percival Decie out at The Moat, and it turned him faint and sick, for he knew at last that ruin stared him in the face. It reached Abishai Abraham, who heard it calmly enough. He gave a few orders quietly, and later in the day the gossips of Westport had further food for scandal, for there was an execution in Sir Percival Decie's house. One instalment of interest on Abishai's loan was overdue—not that this troubled him much, because the hour of his triumph was at hand. Miriam heard this, and straightway made her way to The Moat, intending to confound the schemers and set Sir Percival free.

Meanwhile the Baronet sat at his breakfast-table, holding a note—the note telling him of Armstrong's suspension—in his hand. His face was white and drawn, all his pride shattered by one blow. Victor sat opposite, vague and uneasy, waiting for his father to speak.

"Victor, do you know what this means to us," he said, at length.

"It is very inconvenient, of course," Victor answered, "but nothing to look so tragic about. It is very awkward just now, especially as our outgoings are so heavy; but we must get accommodation elsewhere. Of course we shall have to give some security; but the money must be found, even if we have to deposit the title deeds of The Moat."

"And supposing they are no longer in my possession?"

"Good heavens, we will not suppose anything of the sort! As it is, our position is none too pleasant. But that——Father?"

The mask fell from Sir Percival's face; he leant forward, his face covered with his hands, his whole frame quivering. Not the least of his punishment was the bitter confession he had to make.

"They are not in my possession," he said, in a low voice, which came muffled through his fingers. "I have deceived you, Victor. The Moat has been mortgaged for the past two months."

"And you never told me," Victor said, quietly. It was the only reproach he uttered. "Was I unworthy of your confidence? I might have known."

The Baronet's tones were hoarse as he replied, though his voice trembled with a sound that had in it a suspicion almost of tears, "I thought it better not to speak of it, because I had hoped for brighter things. You do not know how I was pushed, but you do know how everything has gone, locked up in the buildings and pyramids of iron yonder. In addition to my difficulties the bank pulled me up; I had eight-and-forty hours' notice to made a large reduction in my overdraft, and I wanted money then. I went to see Speedwell, but he was powerless to help me; if I had not had the cash in that time I was ruined. There was no time for an ordinary mortgage; Speedwell found a man who would make the advance at once. I went to him and got the money."

"And after that? Go on please, let me hear the worst."

"Then I paid off the overdraft, and started with a large balance to my credit. But that I cannot touch now, and what to do I cannot tell."

There was a long silence between the two men, for it seemed to both of them that there was nothing for it now but ruin. As Victor's eyes roamed round the room, then back to his father seated there, a vague suspicion of the truth shot through him.

"And this creditor of yours?" he asked. "Who is he?"

Sir Percival had been expecting the question and dreading it. Now he began to prevaricate.

"Consider my position," he commented, "consider how I was driven, impelled to make any sacrifice to obtain this money. If I had——"

"Father, is this creditor of yours the man Abraham?"

It was out at last. Sir Percival bowed his head again and groaned.

"I thought so, I felt it," Victor continued, bitterly. "So Speedwell put you into this. Abishai Abraham lent you the money upon the security of The Moat. How generous of him! Was there any further security?"

The last question calmly asked, but not so calmly dwelt upon, struck Sir Percival in a false light. As he hesitated to reply, Victor remembered his visit from Miriam and her strange warning long since forgotten. And yet it had been true, there was some plot on foot, and that in some unknown way connected with a bill of sale. So, as the Baronet made no answer, Victor put the question for himself.

"Was this additional security an unregistered bill of sale?"

"Purely as a matter of form," Sir Percival replied, eagerly. "Of course, I took good care of that, and people like to have as much security as possible. The document, I am informed, is of no practical value."

"As creditors, perhaps not; but between you and Abraham, a deadly weapon. I do not know much about business; but this much I do know, that if there is any arrears of interest due, Abraham can take possession."

Sir Percival's temporary calm forsook him as speedily as it had come.

"You really don't mean that?" he exclaimed. "Why, in that case, I——"

He paused again; but Victor, watching him, fully comprehended the eloquent, ominous silence. For the first time he, too, fell under the ban of despair; his heart sinking under the presentiment of coming trouble.

"In that case, you do owe one instalment. Why not say so at once?"

"How foolish of me!—how extremely foolish of me not to have thought of it before! There was 500 due the day before yesterday; but, of course, we can manage that easily enough."

"Oh, we can manage that," Victor cried, sardonically; but, unless I am mistaken, you will find that failing the punctual payment of interest, the holder of the bill of sale can take possession for the principal sum. Why, oh, why did you not tell me this before? If I had known—if I had only known what that large sum paid in two months ago represented!"

"But don't you think we are premature?" said the Baronet, a little tremulously, awed by this outburst. "Don't you think that with the security he has that Abraham will wait?"

"Wait? Yes; he will wait till it serves his purpose to come here and turn us out into the road. Don't you know he is the hardest-hearted scoundrel in all Westport; that hundreds of people can testify to his cruelty? Wait? Yes; he will wait, and then we are ruined!"

Victor walked to the window to hide the tempest of passion in his face. Away down the drive below he was vaguely conscious of some vehicle approaching, and yet, to his mind, he saw it not.

Sir Percival began, more tremulously than before, "You are looking at the worst side of the case; and, besides, that bill of sale was a pure matter of form. I am not a sanguine man; but I venture to say that Abraham will not presume to come here."

Victor turned from the window with a low, curdling laugh. He took Sir Percival by the arm, and led him to a coign of vantage, where he could see the vehicle now fast approaching the house.

"Look there," he said, "who do you see in that trap yonder? Where the carcase is there shall the eagles be gathered together. Look!"

In the carriage was Abishai and his father, and two other men, the like of which many a good man and true has seen before and trembled at their approach, for the man in possession is a creature apart, and carries his calling written upon him in letters there is no mistaking.

"So much for your sanguine anticipations," continued Victor. "The blow has fallen sooner than even I anticipated. I would give five years of my life to see those faces turned the other way."

But Sir Percival answered not a word. His gold spectacles had fallen from his nose, his hands trembled, his face was white and drawn. Great beads of perspiration stood upon his forehead, or rolled down his haggard features, for the man who had carried fortune upon his shoulders with pride and dignity has dropped down well-nigh helpless under the first breath of trouble. The noise of a bell resounding through the house seemed to strike like a blow at his very heart. He sank into a chair, white and moaning, a heap of black, with his gray head fallen forward on his breast.

"I cannot see them," he moaned. "Great God, it will kill me!"

"You must steel yourself, you will have to see them," Victor answered, cruel only to be kind. "Come, father, it may not be so bad as you think, but for your own sake and mine try and go through the ordeal with dignity. I will go and interview them first."

Fearful almost to trust himself to say more, Victor hurried out, meeting a servant in the doorway. The visitors he found had been shown, after some hesitation, into the library, and in that room he found them.

But if any last lingering hope remained, it was effectually dispelled by one glance at Abishai's distorted face. The money-lender had lashed his hatred till it fairly stung him, and now the sight of his hereditary enemy standing there calm and unmoved, handsome and contemptuous, poured the last drop of oil on the fire of his long smouldering vengeance. Saul Abraham sat in a corner out of sight, dogged and silent; the other two rose, scraped their dingy forelocks, and sat down again, grinning sheepishly.

"Your business here?" Victor demanded, shortly. He expected no quarter, and affected no politeness, knowing that he would gain little by courtesy.

"My business is not with you," Abishai returned, as curtly. "I asked to see Sir Percival Decie, and my determination is not to be trifled with. Fetch him."

"In good time, sir. Meanwhile, I must ask again, what brings you here?"

Abishai leant his chin upon the handle of his crutch, and regarded the speaker with glowing, triumphant eyes. He felt so thoroughly master of the situation that he could afford to indulge in a little pleasantly.

"My business is likely to detain me here for the present," said he. "I have an execution here for 20,501 2s. 11d., amount owing to me under a bill of sale. If you are prepared to hand over the sum mentioned——"

"And supposing I am prepared to pay you that amount forthwith——"

Abishai's jaw dropped; his face became a dull, leaden hue. For a moment he was frightened by his opponent's calm resolution. "In that case," he said, as if grudging his words, "in that case I shall be happy to hand you a receipt, and trouble you no further; also——"

"Also to restore the title deeds of The Moat, a security you have made no effort to realize. But you will not be robbed of your revenge, Mr. Abraham." Abishai's face lightened again. "I call it revenge because I am convinced that you have some vindictive spirit to gratify. It is no mere matter of money, or you would have realised the ample security you hold. But I will not baulk you —the money will not be forthcoming."

Abishai heaved a deep sigh of relief, and a deep growl of satisfaction came from the silent figure of Saul Abraham, behind; even the faces of the other men showed signs of jubilation.

"In that case," said Abishai, "as time is valuable to me, I had better see Sir

Percival at once, and make arrangements to leave these men here. I congratulate you, Mr. Decie, upon your business capabilities. Most people, on painful occasions like these, waste time on idle recriminations."

Victor looked contemptuously at the evil, smiling face, and resisted a strong temptation to strike the speaker. "You shall see Sir Percival," he said; "and as for idle recriminations, one does not waste words on misshapen curs; the task is kept for them. But I am wasting your time. Be good enough to come this way."

At the sound of voices coming nearer, Sir Percival pulled himself together with a violent effort. They found him standing back to the fireplace, calm, cold, and stately, for they could not look into his heart and see the misery and despair that was raging there. In a few words Abishai told his business. Saul Abraham still lingered in the shadows.

"This is a singular breach of faith," Sir Percival commenced. "Really, I had not contemplated this. Sir, you have grossly deceived me!"

Victor felt absolutely grateful for his father's manly demeanour. He crept closer to his side, feeling instinctively that a decisive moment was at hand.

"There is no question of deceit in business matters," Abishai replied, doggedly. "The point is—can you pay the money?"

"To be brief, sir, at this moment I cannot."

Then Abishai raised himself to his full height, his eyes blazing with the fervour of a precious triumph. He pointed with his crutch to the form of Saul Abraham, skulking behind the rest.

"Victor Decie, that man there is what your father made him—a thief, a felon, and an outcast! Your father shall be what I choose to make him! For years I have waited for this moment. I shall not spare you now!"

"He will not spare you now!" Saul Abraham burst out. "Oh, it is good to have a son to avenge his father's wrong. Ay, Sir Percival, you made me what I am. Yes, you can remember; I see it in your eyes! And now I am here in The Moat, and here I stay!"

"Peace!" cried Victor, rushing forward. "Peace, madman! Look here!"

Sir Percival's eyes had gradually closed, then suddenly he swayed backwards, and sank upon his knees, his limbs huddled together as if they had been devoid of life. Victor raised the unconscious form, and carried it tenderly in his arms to a sofa, Abishai looking on fearfully, as if afraid that the cream of his vengeance might be spilt.

"Go on," said Victor, fiercely—"go on, hound! He cannot hear you now!"

"A fair vengeance," Abishai, muttered; "a dispensation of providence. And all brought about by perseverance and honesty."

"Honesty? Who prates of the word here? Honesty? So the eagle says, when he swoops down upon the fold-yard; the fawning hypocrite, who robs the widow and fatherless to increase his own store. Honesty, and Abishai Abraham! Light and darkness good and evil, are things no more remote than that!"

Like the sound of a silver bell, the notes rang through the room. Abishai started back, almost afraid, as if the bitter words had stung him like a thong, for Miriam advanced, a model of living, vivid scorn. On she came till she stood beside the couch; her long white hand fell in a gesture of infinite pity upon the stricken gray head, while with the other she pointed to the hunchback.

"Listen to me," she began again. "Listen while I tell you a plain tale, while I unmask this dastardly plot. You pretend this is a matter of business; you call it also a fair vengeance. Where is your fellow-conspirator, Philip Speedwell that he may hear what I have to say? For months you have schemed to get Sir Percival Decie in your power; but the greed for gain has much to do with this. Cast your memory back, Abishai, to the night when you planned out this thing with Philip Speedwell; how he was to prevent Sir Percival from drawing further money from the bank, and so place him in a position where he would be bound to seek assistance elsewhere. And you were to help him. Then you were to get this place in your possession——"

Gradually Abishai recovered himself as he listened. His quick mind readily understood how disastrous it would be if Miriam was allowed to make further disclosures, and, besides, he was ignorant as to how much she knew. With subtle instinct he fell back upon recrimination.

"This is my sister, gentlemen," he snarled, in a paroxysm of rage; "my virtuous sister, the champion of the oppressed. For this feminite spite we must make necessary allowances. Meanwhile, as you are in the way——"

"Permit me to be the best judge of that," Victor interrupted. "Besides, this conversation interests me. Miss Abraham, pray continue."

"Misshapen in mind; bent, crooked in body and soul," said Miriam, with bitter scorn, "yet he is my brother. I would have tried to shield him, Heaven knows, but he himself has made that impossible. You ask me to reveal the rest of the plot; unfortunately, it is not in my power."

Abishai laughed aloud—a laugh of relief or exultation.

"But this much I do know, that there is something my brother there and Speedwell know of which is valuable to them—something not known to its true owners. It may be minerals, it may be coal; but if I am wrong, I have thought it had something to do with minerals."

"And a really admirable guess, too," said a dry, chuckling voice at this moment.

As they turned round, Signor Sartori, cool and collected, was standing before them. He made the assembled company a grave bow, and, catching sight of Saul Abraham, he motioned him from the room with such a gesture as one throws to a dog.

Mildly he requested that the other two should go likewise, a suggestion which fell in with Abishai's desires. The Professor looked round the room with a smile ere he took up the thread of his previous argument.

"And a really admirable guess, too;" he repeated. "It may be coal, as you say, madam; but it is something far more valuable, being nothing less than— copper." The speaker's pleasant manner changed; his eyes grew very stern as he turned to Abishai. "And you thought to get it, did you, you crook-backed scoundrel!"

The murder was out now. But Abishai did not lack the physical or mental pluck to bear him through the trying situation.

"The law is on my side," said he, showing his yellow teeth in a snarl. "You must prove your words, prove your words. And if I did know there was copper there why should I tell every fool? I defy you all! Turn me out if you can!" A groan from Sir Percival distracted his attention for a moment. "All these things here belong to me; all these things I can sell, and will; and then, Sir Percival Decie, and you, my aristocrat, shall be turned out into the street to starve and rot!"

The Professor smiled. It was just the kind of pantomime in which he delighted. And the others, as they looked into his calm, confident face, drew some comfort and consolation therefrom.

"It is a very pretty programme," said he. "That is, from your point of view. But later on I shall have something to say. Meanwhile, as your presence is rather objectionable, I will ask you to leave us for a while. Go!"

Abishai would have returned the piercing gaze, but his eyes fell. He was conscious of some coming evil; uneasy, moreover, at the Professor's calm air of superiority, the air of one who holds the winning card and knows it. With a sullen scowl he turned, and left the room.

Sartori's manner changed instantly. He walked towards the couch, and, leaning forward, whispered for a few moments in Sir Percival's ear. Gradually, a faint smile broke over his features, followed by a curious agitation; till, at length, he sat up, professing himself better. By the time that Sartori turned to go he was almost himself again.

It was half an hour later before the electro-biologist left the house. On the seashore he encountered Miriam, walking towards Westport listlessly. She was glad to be out in the bright sunshine with the fresh breeze blowing on her cheeks. Sartori, a lover of beauty in the abstract, stopped to walk by her side.

"You are a well-wisher of our friends yonder," he said, at length.

"Yes, or I should not have been there this morning. You have been in Westport long enough to know the story of our lives. You do? Then, does it not seem strange to you that I should like to help the Decies?"

"You can do them the greatest service. Pardon me if I allude to your own history for a moment, but can you find some excuse to go home for an hour? I am not at liberty to go into details now, but this Speedwell has a small safe in his room. This key will fit it. Could you, in the interest of justice and humanity, open that, and bring me all the parchment-covered books you find there? I would not ask you, but——"

"Shall I be helping Sir Percival Decie by so doing?" Miriam asked, looking at the key which the other was holding out temptingly.

"Nothing else, I assure you. Indeed, upon getting these books depends their salvation."

Miriam took the key.

"Then I will do what you want, only I must have some good excuse for going home. If you can give me one——"

"I can. You must ask to see your brother. Probably after the really splendid way you behaved this morning he will possibly refuse to see you, in which case you must send him a message. To a certain extent I am going to take you into my confidence. If your desirable relative refuses to see you, say that your business refers to Lock and Co. You will remember?"

"Is it likely to get him into trouble?"

"It is not calculated to increase his honourable reputation," returned the Professor, cautiously. "Abishai is, I am afraid, but a shady character after all. But let me assure you that you will do him no harm, because——"

The speaker paused abruptly, bit his lip, and swished viciously at the thistles with his cane. He felt that he had been on the verge of a dangerous confidence. "This does not admit of much delay," he continued, "because at the expiration of seven days your brother can sell everything at The Moat. But I can rely upon your nerve, I know. Perhaps, for prudence' sake, we had better part here. And remember Lock and Co. Good morning."

XVII - STRUCK DOWN

For the fortnight which immediately preceded the events narrated in the last chapter, Signor Sartori had not been idle. He had been somewhat disconcerted by the rapidity of Abishai's movements, and now hesitated to play the last card in his hand, for—to quote Bonaparte's famous maxim—the pear was not yet ripe. Unknown to himself fate was fighting upon his side.

The next morning Miriam had seen Hazael. It was too late now to find the money, and even if it could be found, there was no opportunity of replacing it. Speedwell was still nominally manager of the bank; but the provisional liquidator was in occupation. Miriam lingered with Hazael a few moments, administering what comfort she could, then, mindful of Sartori's command, she hastened homeward.

She walked through the shop into the back room with a firm step. Rebecca looked up from the eternal silver she was polishing with no semblance of surprise, or emotion, or even the faintest agitation.

"I am not surprised to see you here," she said, "after yesterday anything from you. And now you come here to taunt us."

"I came here to see Abishai," Miriam answered. "Do you think I would come either with prayers or reproaches! Never! Do you think it is pleasant for me to show my face in the house from which I was turned out into the streets to starve? But enough of this. Where is Abishai?"

A slow, lingering smile broke out on Rebecca's face—the smile of one dwelling upon a pleasing recollection.

"He is in his room, but he will not see you; no, never."

"You think not?" Miriam returned, grimly. "I do."

"He will not yet, anyway, for your friend, Victor Decie, is with him. Yes; he has come to beg for mercy. Ah! I would give something to be there and listen to his pleading words. But Abishai will not listen."

"No; Abishai will not listen," Miriam answered, mechanically. "He will not listen. But you can gratify your curiosity, mother. Go and say to him that I must see him. Say that I am asking nothing for myself; and, if he refuses, then you shall tell him that what I wish to mention concerns him and the firm of Lock and Co. Will you go?"

The natural womanly curiosity overcame the dread in which the mother stood of her elder son, and besides which she had a desire to hear what Victor Decie had to say. With unusual alacrity she put down the metal she was slowly burnishing, and took her way upstairs.

When she returned there seemed to be in her manner an increased respect for Miriam. She motioned her to a chair; but the girl remained standing; she had come with no feelings of friendship or forgiveness.

"Well?" she asked, little doubting the success of Rebecca's mission—"well?"

"He will see you," said Rebecca, rubbing her thin hands together in an ecstacy of satisfaction. "Victor Decie is there, he will remain for perhaps an hour; my Abishai will not spare him. No, no; the hour has come," she turned her keen, piercing eyes upon Miriam. "Who is Lock and Co.?"

"That you will probably know in good time; meanwhile I will wait. I suppose I may be permitted to go up to my old room?"

Rebecca answered not, still rubbing her hands together and smiling in a feline manner unpleasant to behold. Miriam, taking silence for consent, turned away and walked quietly upstairs. There was nothing to be heard, save the high-pitched voices from Abishai's apartment; not a soul stirring till she came to the door of Speedwell's room. She tried the latch, and it yielded to her hand. A moment later she had shut herself inside.

All too soon had come the golden opportunity. She had the little key in her hand; the iron safe Sartori had mentioned lay in one corner by the wall. For a brief moment Miriam hesitated, then she steeled herself again. She knelt down, and, with fingers shaking a little turned the key in the lock, and raised the heavy lid as she looked in.

First she turned out a confused mass of papers, then some oblong volumes bound in half-calf—account-books evidently—and so on till she had almost emptied the safe. Nearly at the bottom she came upon two parchment-covered bank books, marked 'Lock ad Co.'; also a long, thin volume, bearing in gilt letters 'L. and Co.' Nothing more bearing the same imprint. Carefully she replaced the scattered papers one by one. Her heart was beating wildly now; but, at last, they were all safely stowed away, the strong box locked again. A moment later she was creeping downstairs; then, in a fit of sudden resolve, she crept through the shop out into the street.

For she had determined to find Sartori without loss of time. As she walked along she found herself wondering in a vague way what connection the travelling professor could have with the exclusive family of Decie. But such speculations were cut short by meeting the object of her search near the Angel, where he was now staying. He took of his hat with a flourish, smiling gallantly as he did so, but at the sight of her grave face he checked the rising compliment, and assumed a business-like air.

"And those," he asked, pointing to the volumes—"those are the books?"

"Yes," said Miriam, quickly, with no shadow of triumph in her tones. "They are."

"Then allow me to congratulate you upon being one of the most remarkable women I have ever met. 'Neminem sapientionen unto quam Socratem'—which remark is not so egotistical as it seems—but, really, your promptitude puts my poor efforts to the blush. You have done a most excellent morning's work, Miss Abraham. If you will accompany me I will tell you a little more."

So saying, the Professor led the way through the hotel into his private room, for Westport had inclined favourably to his entertainment, and the tide of his prosperity was at flood. He motioned his visitor to a chair, and laid his hand upon the books which she had placed upon the table.

"In the first place," said he. "I am going to take you a little further into my confidence. Probably you have wondered why I display such an interest in the fortunes of the Decies. Well, I have more than one reason—the first being that I am fond of playing the amateur detective, and I have matched my wits against the two most cunning scoundrels in Christendom—the one being Philip Speedwell, the other, truth compels me to state, is your admirable brother, Abishai. Now, if I understand aright, there is a long-standing and bitter feud between your family and my—I mean the Decies; a feeling I am pleased to see you do not share. Probably you think this unfortunate affair over at The Moat is dictated by vengeance alone."

"Not quite," Miriam smiled. "There is some object to gain besides."

"Perfectly right, my dear young lady, and that object, in a single word, is copper. The waste lands round the Old Meadows, which form part of The

Moat estate, contain some of the richest copper veins in the kingdom; so the astute Abishai, and the equally astute Speedwell, put their heads together, and up to now, from their point of view, the result is eminently satisfactory."

"But I do not altogether understand yet how they will benefit."

"Time, my dear young lady, will elucidate the mystery," the Professor interrupted, indicating that space by a wave of his hand. "But if Sir Percival cannot find the money, your brother will foreclose, and thus gratify his lust for vengeance, and make himself a millionaire at the same time."

"But surely, if this copper vein is so valuable, it would be easy enough to find some honest capitalist who would pay off the encumbrance? If you were to go to Mr. Lockwood——"

"Really, you are a remarkable young lady," quoth the Professor, admiringly. "But at the present moment Lockwood is powerless; all his available capital was deposited in Armstrong's Bank to meet a cheque for payment of a large property; besides which, any outside interference would upset my delicately-laid schemes. But we have gone off at a tangent. I was about to tell you why I am so deeply interested in the fortunes of the Decies. You, of course, know the history of that direful quarrel, and the unworthy cause thereof? Equally, of course, you know of Captain Decie, who, by the way, was a shocking bad lot. Well, to resume. In the first place, this Captain Decie is alive."

"Indeed!" said Miriam, interestedly. "And do you know him?"

"Intimately; I may say he is the best friend I have. Now I am going to surprise you; but you must keep the secret. I am Captain Decie."

Miriam's astonishment left her no room for words.

The quondam Professor resumed, ere she had sufficiently recovered to speak, "Yes, I am the erring prodigal, as your father could tell you if he liked; he was the only one who recognised me, but I am not afraid of his betraying me. As to the rest of my plan it must develop itself. You must leave these little volumes with me, and in good time you shall know all. But Philip Speedwell and Abishai Abrahams, you may rest assured, will never draw one single farthing from the Old Meadow Copper Mines."

All Trevor Decie's light airy badinage had fallen away, leaving his face and mien stern and uncompromising. He felt no mercy now for the scoundrels' fate, whom his own skill had placed in his power, and Miriam, looking up, noted the change which had come upon him. For the first time she wondered and feared, with a rush of sisterly feeling, whether she had placed Abishai in danger.

"And my brother—Abishai," Miriam broke the silence—"will he be safe?"

"I hope so," Decie returned, through his set teeth; "safe in gaol. And now you had better go back to him. Invent some pretext for speaking to him. I would not for the mines of Golconda that he took alarm."

Miriam's thoughts were painful and confused as she turned her feet homeward.

What had she done in her zeal for the Decies? Deciding rapidly, as she always did, she determined to warn Abishai ere it was too late. Just then her thoughts were interrupted by the vision of Victor Decie coming rapidly down the street. His face was pale. His eyes glared, but with no gleam of recognition there. Impulsively Miriam laid her hand upon his arm. He passed by, as if conscious of nothing save some unseen horrid spectre, hidden to all eyes but his own.

Rebecca was still polishing her silver with a patience which never seemed to tire. To Miriam's question if Abishai was still in his room she nodded grimly.

"Yes, and young Decie has gone. But not until after a violent quarrel. I crept up the stairs and listened. Abishai never spared him—my noble boy! Presently I shall see him, and he will tell me all. But I dare not disturb him now. But you should have seen the young man's face as he went out. It was like death—like despair."

Miriam lingered to hear no more. The despair, if her late confidant's face was any index, threatened to be by no means on one side only. Abishai must be warned at once. She walked slowly up the stairs, and knocked at the closed door. No answer came, and she walked in.

Abishai was leaning over his table; there was money lying there, and parchments of various kinds. Miriam touched him on the shoulder, but he heeded not; she spoke to him, but he did not reply, his attitude one of perfect stillness. His head had fallen on one side.

"Abishai, I wish to speak to you?"

Still no answer, the words sounding strangely in the stillness. A bright sunray fell through the uncurtained window, lighting up a red stain upon the table, upon the still man's pallid face. There was a rent high upon his breast, through which a thin stream of blood oozed clammily. Abishai had been murdered in the hour of triumph, foully slain, and Victor Decie, driven to madness, had done this direful thing!

XVIII - HE IS THE MAN

Hideous in life, how much more hideous in death? There was a smile upon the scarce-cold features, bitter and contemptuous, the last relict of a lost soul. He must have been stricken with awful swiftness, for there was no sign of a struggle even—nothing save the gaping rent and the red stream upon the bare floor to show the trace of crime. For a moment Miriam stood horror-stricken, regarding the fearful thing in fascinated awe. Then shriek after shriek burst from her lips.

Rebecca downstairs, polishing the silver and gloating over the coming downfall of the Decies, heard her and wondered. The sounds came again; and fearful of something, she hurried upstairs. She found Miriam standing like a chill white statue, pointing silently to the still form seated at the table.

"Abishai," she cried—"Abishai, my son, what is this?"

But no answer came.

Rebecca knelt down and took one cold hand in her own. Its coldness chilled her; thrilled it as if he had been burning. Her fingers wandering upwards, became wet with the thick blood, and as she looked at them, she seemed to know what had happened. The gash over the heart caught her eye, then the dead white face. For a moment she knelt, looking up imploringly, as if the intensity of her pleading could call back the lost soul to the stiffening clay. In her eyes were no tears, on her features no trace of sadness or lamentation; but all the worst passions of nature crystallized into determination and resolve.

"Another life," she said, rising to her feet—"another life taken by them. First a husband's disgrace, and now a son's existence. If I had only known—if I had only known when they were quarrelling. If I had only known!"

Each reproach came fainter than the last, but more intensified and slowly.

Miriam had remained, still hearing nothing, and now the words seemed to float round the room till they reached her understanding, and fitted themselves together like the pieces of a puzzle.

She realized now how dangerous was the position in which Victor Decie stood. What he owed to the dead man; how they had parted with bitter words and recrimination; and, lastly, the memory of his face as it came back to her. All was remembered now.

"It is idle standing there," said she, in a strangely-calm voice; "we must do something. Rouse yourself, mother! Scream or cry! Do anything but look like that!"

Slowly Rebecca aroused herself. A panther-like look had come over her face, but she neither screamed nor wept. As yet she had not realized it.

"Yes, we must do something—we must find the murderer. Ah! we shall not have far to look, Miriam. Will you take his part now?"

"I shall not be one to shield the man who did that thing, you might know that. Come! let us get away—the sight sickens me. Mother, why do you look like that? Surely you don't suspect——"

"I suspect nothing; I am certain. Victor Decie struck the blow that killed my boy, sure as I am his mother. Did I not hear the quarrel?—did I not see the murderer's face as he went away? Fool that I was to call it despair, when, after all, it was murder. Call in the neighbours," Rebecca cried, with rising passion —"call them in, and show them the cowardly deed he has done! Show them a gentleman's vengeance. My poor, dead boy!"

She threw herself upon the corpse, in an ecstacy of grief, holding it tenderly withal. Miriam dashed down the stairs and out into the street; opposite a policeman on duty was passing, and, in answer to her call, he stopped. Before her wildness and the majesty of her beauty his officialism melted away. He so far forgot himself as to smile.

"Nothing serious, I hope," he said, in answer to her summons.

Like most of her people in the district he knew her, and her story.

"More than serious. Murder has been done in our house; done in the open daylight. Come with me at once."

All the officer's gaiety of manner vanished. He turned across the road swiftly, and, following his guide, passed into the house and up the stairs. With the stolidity of his class he made a swift ocular examination of the body, then asked if anything had been disturbed.

"I must trouble you to leave this room," he said, with a satisfied nod at Miriam's negative answer, "and you must allow me to put the key in my pocket. This is a serious case; the inspector must know of it at once. And if I can do anything for you, miss——"

"Indeed, you can," Miriam exclaimed, gratefully. "If you will walk, or send down to Armstrong's bank, and ask Mr. Speedwell and my brother to come up at once, I shall be thankful."

The officer bowed and retired, walking along the street without his official and customary dignity. It seemed ages to Miriam waiting there before the wished-for arrivals came. The silence was oppressive; Miriam standing in the doorway, her ear strained to catch the slightest sign; Rebecca thrown back in her chair, muttering scraps of broken curses and lamentation from time to time. Presently Speedwell and Hazael came in. The reaction was more than the girl could bear. She threw herself into Hazael's arms, and sobbed with heartbreaking violence.

"We know nothing," said Hazael, when the first storm of grief had worn away. "We were told we were urgently required at home. What is it?"

"Abishai is dead," Miriam answered, simply. Speedwell started violently.

"Great heavens," he exclaimed, "dead!"

"Dead! say murdered! Ay! you may stare, all of you; murdered—I say—murdered! murdered!" Rebecca cried, till the words rang in the roof. "In his own house, in his own room, in open daylight. And I let the assassin escape; I let him go by me out into the street, when I might have held him till the police came and took him away safely."

Hazael and Speedwell looked to Miriam for explanations.

"Mr. Victor Decie has been here this morning. He and Abishai had a violent quarrel, which mother partly overheard. Then I came here directly he was gone, and went upstairs to see Abishai, and found——"

She stopped, covering her face with trembling fingers, unable to say more.

"And you found him dead," said Speedwell, impatiently. "Try and control yourself."

"Yes, I found him dead, killed by a knife thrust in the heart. I cannot tell you any more. What do you think of it?"

"Have you seen Decie since?" Speedwell asked

"Yes; singularly enough I met him. He—he seemed disturbed—so disturbed, that he did not know me."

"He has been with us since then. I noticed his appearance; indeed, I asked him if he was ill. But he only passed his hand across his forehead and answered something. If he had not been a Decie," Speedwell concluded, with a thin sneer, "I should have suspected him of intoxication. Miriam, this is important; even aristocrats sometimes indulge in vulgar crime——"

The conclusion of this sentence was lost to history by the arrival of the police inspector, who entered unceremoniously at that moment. His conversation was brief to taciturnity, nipping all Speedwell's loquacious suggestion in the bud. What he wanted, he said, was to see the body and make an examination of the room. In this he was accompanied by both Hazael and Speedwell. Miriam could hear the sound of heavy footsteps tramping across the bare floor, and even catch the subdued hum of conversation going on between the trio. Two policemen loitered on the doorstep, attended by a small crowd of the curious in such matters, whom the sight of the blue coats and helmets had gathered there. In the midst of the confusion a customer walked into the shop, and stood impatiently tapping his umbrella upon the floor for some time before he attracted Miriam's attention. To her surprise she found it to be Captain Decie, better known as Professor Sartori.

He recognised her with a nod and a meaning smile.

"I knew you were here," he said. "I have been waiting for you nearly an hour, so I became impatient, and here I am. By the presence of these guardians of the law there must be something wrong. Perhaps the estimable Abishai——"

"You should not have come here," Miriam whispered, hurriedly. "Have you not heard? Abishai is dead."

"Dead?" exclaimed the Professor. "You don't say so! How disappointing!"

"Oh, hush—hush! You don't know what you are saying! It is worse than death; it is murder! I will try and see you presently, if you wish to see me."

And Miriam explained briefly and rapidly the startling events of the morning.

For once in his life the listener was seriously disconcerted. There was a troubled look on his face as he heard what was said, especially as regarded the visit of his nephew to the murdered man, and confessed to himself that appearances were greatly against him.

"Can you see me presently," he asked, at length, "if only for half an hour? Your people are pretty certain to apply for a warrant against Victor—that is, if they are allowed to do so pending the inquest. And Victor is away——"

"Away at this moment? Why, his presence in Westport is absolutely necessary for the sake of his reputation. Telegraph at once."

"Unfortunately, it is too late. By this time he is not in the country even. He won't be able to get back here under four days at the least; and this to happen just now, when everything——"

"That will do," Miriam interrupted, hurriedly; "they are coming downstairs now. I will meet you in an hour at the corner of the street. Go."

The inspector's face was very stem, and his questions more brief than ever. In a few words he elucidated from Rebecca all she had seen that morning. With a short "Good morning!" he was gone, leaving his officers behind. For a time there was an ominous silence. Hazael's face was strangely troubled. Speedwell wore a look of triumph he tried in vain to hide.

"What did he think, Hazael?" Miriam asked, with hesitation.

"There is no occasion to think," Speedwell interrupted; "the thing is clear as daylight. Decie came here to ask for time, or favour of some kind, and Abishai refused. Then they quarrelled, and Decie struck the fatal blow. In my mind there is no cause for doubt."

But Hazael answered not, still wearing that strangely troubled look. As Miriam turned her eyes reproachfully upon him, he strove to throw the feeling aside. Presently he spoke in a strange, hard voice.

"I would not like to go so far as that. It is an awful accusation to make against a fellow-creature upon such slight evidence. Circumstantial evidence, perfect as it looks, is liable to break down, and, for aught we know, the real criminal may be in the house now."

Hazael had spoken those words with visible effort, scarce knowing what he had been saying. Miriam's quick eye had noticed his perturbation, but Speedwell had turned away to hide a certain pleased look he would fain have kept from Miriam's contemplation.

"I agree with Hazael," Miriam observed. "I cannot believe Victor Decie capable of such a crime. He could not do it!"

"He has an ardent supporter," said Speedwell, with his thin sneer. "I might have remembered the liking, to put it mildly, you have for him. Meanwhile, till something more probable turns up, I prefer to hold to my original opinion."

So saying the speaker lounged out, and turned his steps in the direction of the bank. The tragedy, save so far as it affected certain cut and dried schemes of his, troubled him not a whit. Miriam looked after the retreating form with flashing eyes. To her the taunt at such a time was peculiarly coarse and cruel. Hazael had wandered listlessly into the shop, and thither Miriam followed him —she scare knew why, save the natural desire for company at such a moment.

"Hazael," she exclaimed, suddenly, "do you hear a noise overhead?"

Hazael started. Of late it had taken little to startle his overstrung nerves. Now he listened, plainly hearing something like a stealthy footstep. He was almost afraid to trust his voice, yet managed to answer lightly that he heard nothing. Miriam turned from him, and assumed a listening attitude. It came again, so clearly and distinct that Hazael, in spite of his assumed indifference, could no longer feign deafness.

"Perhaps it is mother walking overhead," he ventured.

For answer, Miriam pointed to the crouching figure seen in the half-light of the little sitting-room. Her face was white, but not whiter, nothing like so agitated, as the features of her companion.

"I must know what it is. Stay while I go and see."

Hazael sprang forward, and held her back.

"You shall not go!" he whispered, hoarsely. "You must not go! There might be danger for you! No, no; better stay where you are; and it—it may be fancy!"

He was regarding her in an agony of fear. Great beads of perspiration ran down his face. His hands, laid upon her shoulders, trembled. As they stood there, his painful intensity of feeling seemed to be conveyed in some strange magnetic way to Miriam, for a huge fear was gathered at her heart.

"Hazael, what ails you? What do you know, that you are concealing from me? Surely you do not know who did this thing?" Suddenly she remembered the money scattered about the dead man's table. "Perhaps in a moment of temptation. Hazael, what do you know?"

"That Victor Decie is innocent. Is not that enough?"

"It is not enough. You know more—you know who the culprit is!"

"Heaven help me!" Hazael groaned. "I am afraid I do!"

Miriam paused in astonishment, unable to reply. The stealthy footstep came again, seeming so loud in the strained stillness that the girl found herself wondering that the quiet figure half turned in the gloom yonder, could not hear. Her curiosity and her high courage were aroused. Now was the time to discover the mystery, if mystery there was. Hazael, as the sounds smote upon his ear again, had fallen, half fainting, against a chair. Without, another word, Miriam turned from him, and walking with steps as stealthily as those overhead, quickly crept up the stairs.

For a full quarter of an hour she was gone. Hazael began to breathe more freely. The leaden hue died out of his face, and a little colour crept in. He felt a wild, exhilarating feeling of relief, a feeling all too short-lived, for Miriam was with him again, her eyes lighted up with wild excitement.

"Come with me," she whispered. "Now I understand why you were afraid. But you had no cause to fear. Come! you were wrong—doubly wrong and wicked to doubt. Come! I must have a witness."

And with a new courage, born of hope, he went.

The quondam Professor, waiting anxiously at the corner of the street, marvelled to see the brilliant bloom on Miriam's cheeks as she came, with swift feet, towards him. There was a lightness in her step, a wealth of hope in her glorious eyes, which was surely the harbinger of great good fortune. Hazael lagged behind, like a man who has suddenly awaked from an evil dream, to find that life was bright before him yet.

"You have something to tell me," said the Professor, blandly. "By your appearance you have discovered something. Wonderful young lady!"

"Yes, I have discovered something," Miriam exclaimed, laughing and crying in a breath; "and I have a witness here—my brother." She indicated the still dreaming Hazael. "He will bear me out. And Victor is innocent."

"And you love him," murmured Decie, under his breath. "You want me to tell you where my—ahem!—young Sir Galahad has gone. Really, you have no idea how awkward it is. Come a little aside with me. Well, Victor has gone to Hull, en route for Rotterdam, on business which intimately concerns Messrs. Lock and Co. He will be away a week."

"And by that time will be denounced as my brother's assassin. There is no time to lose; you must fetch him back at once."

"Impossible!" exclaimed the Professor, in dismay. "My presence here is absolutely necessary. I am expecting a detective here every hour. A day's absence will ruin not only my plans, but Sir Percival's too."

Miriam hesitated for a moment, with a great holiness of purpose shining in her eyes. "Very well," she said, "you must stay. Give me your nephew's address in Rotterdam. No words, sir, for expostulations will be useless. What I can prove remains to be seen; but I shall cross to Rotterdam myself to-night. I may even be able to catch him before he leaves."

"And the inquest," said Hazael, "fixed for tomorrow. Are you mad?"

XIX - INTO THAT SILENT SEA

Wild as was Miriam's resolve, once determined, no power could shake her resolution. By the merest accident she had fallen upon an important clue, intangible as yet; but the thought of clearing Victor's name—the bare idea of being the first, not only to warn him of his peril, but also to give him hope and courage—was dangerously sweet. And, moreover, Trevor Decie, turning matters over in his mind, concluded that there was no reason why this thing should not be done. Sir Percival was far too prostrated to leave home at present, and the quondam Professor, in his character of chief conspirator, felt that his presence was absolutely necessary in Westport. Now that Abishai had met this violent end, he feared Speedwell's disappearance. It was no time, therefore, to study appearances.

As Miriam speeded away towards Hull, she gradually noticed a change in the weather. For some days it had been calm and still; now the sky was piled up with angry clouds; an ominous wind swept through the forest trees. The storm passed away inland, leaving the sky leaden and the landscape swept by the rushing wind. As the cornlands sloped away to long marshes and sand reaches there was occasionally a glimpse of dark, tossing water, touched here and there by hissing crests of foam.

Even in the busy docks, sheltered by solid masonry from the storm-lashed waves, the shipping rose and fell gently, as if actuated by a hidden sympathy.

It had grown quite dark by this time; the long stretch of quays lighted here and there with lanterns, and ship's lights flickering in the wind, The steam was streaming in a broken wreath from the funnels of a boat lying a little away from the rest; there was a little knot of muffled passengers standing in the lane of light waiting for the last moment, and gazing anxiously heavenward for the promise of the night. This was the Rotterdam packet, waiting now for the mails.

Miriam had taken her ticket, and gone aboard. She felt strangely lonely in the crowd, for it was summer time, and many were crossing besides those compelled by business or duty. More than one eye was cast admiringly at that tall, queenly figure against the rail, watching the reflection of the lights below, and listening to the angry rush of waters outside.

A tremor ran through the little vessel from stem to stern, as she swung slowly round. There was a faint throb, a churning of waters, a passing glimpse of feathery foam, shining red in the lessening lantern lights; a gradual upheaving of the deck, and they were away. It seemed as if everything on the shore was reeling to and fro in the throes of an earthquake, till gradually the lights died away and everything was swallowed up in a waste of angry waters.

Through the dark night the wind shrieked and whistled in the cordage, the decks were wet with spray, and when morning dawned slowly, as if unwilling to wake upon such a scene, there was still the monotonous sweep of leaden waves, white crested under the wild morning sky. It seemed ages till in the hazy distance a long low line broke the horizon, and gradually began to take shape, till at last a gleam of transient sunshine shot out of the dark heavens, and Miriam saw that her weary journey was at an end.

It seemed all strange and wild to her, faint as she was with hunger and want of sleep. The startling events of the previous day, the recollection of Abishai as she had found him, and now the strange, quaint town, all so new and novel, gave her a queer, dreamy feeling of mocking unreality. She found at length, by inquiry of the fellow passengers, the hotel she was in search of, where she discovered Victor Decie had a private room. When she arrived he was not in, but she made them understand what she wanted. The queer up and down motion of the boat made her dizzy still; the chair she had thrown herself into was comfortable. Gradually remembrance fell away from her and she slept.

When she awoke again it was with a pleasant feeling of renewed strength and vigor. Scarcely had she time to realize her position, when the door opened and Victor Decie came in. For a moment he rubbed his eyes in astonishment; then came towards her with outstretched hand.

"Miss Abraham! Can I believe my eyes? I have only been a few hours here, and already the sight of a familiar face is positively refreshing."

Evidently he knew nothing. The strained wildness Miriam had noted on his face when last they had met was gone, there was a ring of hope, almost of exultation, in his voice. As Miriam clasped his hand, a thrill seemed to run through her frame, and the blood mounted to her face. She had come on his business and he was glad to see her. That in itself was recompense enough for all she had done.

"Then you have heard nothing?"

"I have heard a great deal," Victor replied, brightly. "I have already found out sufficient to convict Speedwell, and——But I forget. You can know nothing of this."

"And my brother, you would say. No harm can come to him now. He is dead."

"Dead! Why, only yesterday morning I was with him."

There was no trace of guilt or hesitation on his face; nothing but blank amazement.

"And that is why I am here," Miriam continued. "Yesterday morning you were with him. You came, I apprehend, to ask for some little grace?"

"I confess I was sanguine enough—call it foolish, if you like—to hope for some little quarter; but I was mistaken. I had not reckoned what a passion this money-making becomes. And we had a violent quarrel."

He paused abruptly, for there was something in Miriam's face which frightened him. She saw the look reflected there, and rising, laid her hand upon his arm. All the passion of her nature began to run like quicksilver through her veins.

"You had a violent quarrel," she said, stifling her feelings ruthlessly. "You even went so far as to threaten him. Yes; that was heard. I met you looking like a madman just afterwards, with something written in your face which frightened me. Straight from seeing you I went to Abishai, only to find him—dead."

"And you think that our quarrel had something to do with this?"

"I think so? Never! But others do. You do not understand. My brother did not die a natural death; he was murdered. And you had been heard to quarrel with him, and others saw your agitation besides me; and you have left Westport suddenly, and I have come to save you."

"I am accused of this monstrous crime?" Victor cried, aghast. "Preposterous! absurd! They must be mad to say such a thing. So you have come over to warn me. Really I do not know how to thank you. Perhaps you will suggest some course, some disguise, by which I may be safe from detection."

Miriam winced under the mocking irony of his words, as if he had struck her a sudden blow. The rose pink crept into her face again; her eyes filled with tears.

"Do not speak to me like that," she said, humbly. "I cannot bear them from you. I—I did it for the best, out of love for you. Yes; you may be surprised, but if I had not loved you, I should not be here now."

The carefully-guarded secret was out after all these years. It was Victor's turn to colour now like a love-sick girl. Yet he was touched by this abnegation of self, and the feeling which had prompted such a sacrifice. With all his high sense of honour, he was but a man, and the girl standing opposite to him was perilously beautiful in her sweet confusion.

"Forgive me," he said, more gently. "I might have known that you were acting for the best; but you surprised me, you horrified me by your declaration. Believe me, I am grateful—the more now that I comprehend the danger in which I stand. What am I to do?"

The graveness of these words recalled Miriam to her sense of duty. For a brief moment she had been carried away by passion. Now she was a very woman again.

"There is but one thing to do, and that is, to return home at once. Indeed, any delay may be dangerous. Ah! they little know who the culprit is."

"Do you know," Victor demanded, swiftly. "Do you know."

"I think so—I fear so. Westport will have a dish of horrors to gloat over. But, Mr. Decie, cannot you see the necessity of getting home at once?"

Victor was silent. Up to the present his business in Rotterdam had been progressing marvellously well. And now, in the eleventh hour, his triumph threatened to be snatched away from him. He hesitated, half convinced, and listening in a vague way to the hiss of the rain pouring against the small, thick window panes, and the wind roaring in the chimneys.

"Miss Abrahams,"—he broke the silence at length—"do you know why I came here?

"Partly, yes. Your—I should say, the Professor, has enlightened me to a certain extent. Indeed, I may say I have been an instrument in his hands."

"I came here so that I might be prepared to unmask a couple of scoundrels. In one case the decree of Providence has taken justice out of my hands; in the other case, there is yet time. I am not doing this from any sordid or revengeful motives, but simply for my father's sake—ay, and for the sake of hundreds of sufferers besides. I am on the horns of a dilemma. If I go home now I shall clear my character at the expense of my patrimony. Cannot this remain for another day?"

"Surely you know your own business best," Miriam answered, wearily. "I do not see that a day is, after all, imperative. Complete your indictment, and we will go home together; and I will complete mine."

It was a strange night and day that followed. Miriam wandered about the quaint old town heedless of the driving rain and storm which swept inland from the sea with a mighty blast and roar, as if it would tear down the work of man's hands. Victor was away transacting his business, and when Miriam chanced to see him he was moody and preoccupied, eager to complete his task, and still more eager to get home again.

Late the following evening he burst in, wild and excited. At last he had done. As he came in another great gust of wind drove against the windows, lashing the swirling rain against them in sheets and volleys, with a rattle like the roar of artillery.

"I have finished!" he exclaimed. "We can return to-night."

Miriam looked out at the angry, broken sky, fast darkening in the coming night —a wild, tempestuous night, with the demons of discord riding on the storm.

"We shall have a dangerous passage," she said.

"Not so dangerous; the look of things is deceptive," he replied. "I would not miss returning to-night though it were twice as rough and stormy. We must have no more delay how. See what I have here."

Victor produced a pocket-book with steel clasps, strongly bound in oiled silk. He laid it upon the table with a proud air of triumph.

"Do you know what that contains?" he continued. "But of course you don't. In there I have proof clear as day of more than one man's perfidy. You have spoken of Lock and Co. Do you know the firm actually consisted of your brother and Philip Speedwell? But you will hear everything in time. And now do you feel bold enough to cross to-night, or will you prefer to wait?"

"I will go with you," said Miriam, "I am not afraid."

She spoke truly, she had never known what it was to fear. Moreover, the thought of the lonely hours she was to spend with Victor Decie was inexpressibly sweet. What mattered then a little discomfort, or, for the matter of that, danger either. Victor looked at her admiringly.

"Few who were not forced to go would care to cross to-night. Come, we have not time to waste; it is almost dark now. Listen to that."

The hurricane struck the house again, making it rock and tremble to the very foundations, while the rain dashed against the windows in blinding sheets, like finely broken spray.

On the quay the force of the gale was so great as to render conversation impossible. Save for the sailors of the outgoing packets, clad in their oilskins, and looking skyward with grave, earnest faces, no sign of human life was visible. Overheard the clouds rolled like an inky pall driven before the hurricane. The captain stood calmly watching the final preparation; on his bronzed, weather-beaten face came a look of transient surprise as he noticed the presence of his passengers.

"You are a bold man, sir," he said, with a touch of the gale in his voice. "Few folks would care to face the sea we shall have to-night."

Victor nodded, and smiled in reply, unable to make himself heard in the voluminous roar. Suddenly there came a lull in the storm, though it still seemed to thrill and rumble in their ears. So it continued for a time, till they had pushed out to sea, and the blurred misty light had faded behind them.

"I would rather remain on deck, if we may," Miriam answered, in reply to a question from Victor. "I should feel suffocated down below."

The sea still ran high, and rushed occasionally in an impetuous wave over the decks. Victor had wrapped himself and his companion in a waterproof-lined cloak, under which they talked and whispered through the night. Gradually the wind spurted again, coming stronger in long, fitful gusts. Every timber in the brave little vessel creaked and groaned against the onslaught of the pitiless sea. Higher and higher it came as they lay to, with engines going at half speed, for now there was no disguising it longer; they were fighting for life, and every soul on board knew it.

"You are not frightened?" Victor asked.

"No, I am not frightened," Miriam answered.

She felt a strange, blissful security in the nearness of his presence. His one arm was thrown round her, as they were drawn together by the common danger which levels all distinctions of race or class. For a time they were silent, till a faint, feeble thrill, followed by a jerky pause, startled them. The boat heeled over for a moment and broached to. The screw shaft had broken.

If there had been hope before, they knew there was none now. The heavy seas which had hitherto struck them upon the bows now began to pitch heavily from the stern. With much difficulty Victor contrived to lash himself and his companion to an iron stanchion. Scarcely had he done this, when the captain reeled by, and stopped to cheer them for a moment.

"You are all right?" he asked, leaning forward. "Yes, we are in great danger. No reason to disguise it now. The engine shaft has broken. We are in man's hands no longer. God bless you, sir."

There was something in the seaman's eyes besides salt water. A moment later and he was gone. A great wave struck the ship, washing her from stem to stern. Above all the wild, maddening roar a piercing cry went up. What it was they could only shudder and conjecture.

A wild, passionate protest warred in Victor's heart. It seemed hard, so hard, to die thus in the moment of victory. His petulant anger died away, and an infinite pity and tenderness for the girl by his side succeeded.

"How can you forgive me?" he cried, laying his lips upon her ear. "Miriam, how can you forgive me for bringing you to this?"

At the sound of her name Miriam raised her arms and wound them round his neck. They were together now. She had him to herself, and nothing but death could part them. In a sudden impulse she kissed him, for there could be no shame in her love now—kissed him, not despairingly, but with a wild exultation and a fierce delight strangely unnatural.

"There is nothing to forgive," said she. "Am I not repaid, ay, twenty-fold? It is no self-abnegation which impelled me to do this thing. I did it because I love you. Why should I not say so?—why should I be ashamed of that? Kiss me! kiss me! if only once, Victor; then I can die happy."

She was cold, wet, drenched to the skin; her face lashed by the stinging spray and foam, yet there was a warmth at her heart, a glow upon her lips which defied the pitiless storm. She felt a pride in her confession—a pride no sense of shame could take away. For answer Victor bent and kissed her lips, long and tenderly. The wind roared and raged, but she heard it not.

Morn had commenced to break in the eastern sky, throwing up long shafts of angry crimson, glowing on the broken masts and streaming cordage. As the doomed ship plunged and rolled, rising upon the crests, they could see a faint blue outline far ahead, though too near, as they drifted onward. Gradually the light grew stronger with the rising day; the distant coastline became more strongly marked, till at length the watchers could make out wooded hills, with a long white house, with lawns sweeping from the shore, where, early as it was, a group of men were watching the doomed barque.

"Surely I cannot be mistaken," Victor cried. "It must be, it is The Moat. The irony of fate! To be drowned in sight of one's own home."

Scarcely had the words left his mouth when the keel grated, and, throwing up her bows in one mad, despairing plunge, the vessel flung herself forward upon the rocks. Slowly she heeled over, leaving the portion of the deck upon which Miriam and Victor were fastened high out of the water. A great wave washed the whole length, and when its force was spent, they were alone.

"Ten minutes, five minutes more—and then——" Victor covered his face with his hands. "Oh, it is hard, it is very hard, to die now!"

The tide was falling, though the sea still made a clean breach over the barque. Presently a rocket, pallid in the increasing light, passed over them, but the line fell wide. Another tremendous sea struck them; another such and she must part. Miriam had dexterously unbound the cord which fettered them, and tried to rise to her feet. Another rocket, better aimed than the last, fell within reach. As swiftly as his cramped fingers allowed Victor hauled in the line, and fixed the rope to the iron stanchion. Another wave; another like that and it would be too late. Already the line had tightened, making a pathway of safety to the shore.

"Go," Victor commanded, pointing to the life buoy. "Go, and perchance there may be yet time for me."

"No, there will be no time, you know that. I shall stay here; your life is more valuable than mine. Victor, listen to me," for he had turned away impatiently; "I have done much for you."

"Heaven knows you have. Forgive me, but——"

"Then once more kiss me, and remember that I——"

She threw her arms around his neck, and held his face down to hers. Then fiercely she thrust him away, and rising, pushed the cloak aside. There was a white flash as her hands went up, a pleading smile on her lips; then straight as an arrow she cast herself into the raging hell of waters.

The life buoy came within reach. Victor clutched it wildly, dazed and stunned, but with a desire for life strong within him. Half way to the shore something snapped, and he was battling with the waves. But gradually strong hands dragged him onwards out of the seething cauldron, above the reach of the hungry waters, and he was saved.

XX - CONFIRMATION STRONG

They had removed the unfortunate hunchback in the meantime for the convenience of the inquest, and then, after solemn deliberation, they had returned a verdict of 'Wilful murder' against Victor Decie. On the day following the tragedy there had been a preliminary inquiry, almost immediately adjourned, pending the presence of two most important witnesses —Victor Decie and Miriam. Probably the police had been properly assured that no attempt on the former's part had been contemplated, for there was an air of mystery about their movements which puzzled the quidnuncs and Philip Speedwell not a little. Hazael had said nothing. He had waited for Miriam's return, and now all Westport knew that she was beyond the reach of earthly cross-examination.

Victor was little the worse next day for his adventure. The sea had gone down to its shining summer beauty, but it had not given up its dead. He wandered the next morning along the sands, but ever and anon there came into his eyes a mistiness suspiciously like tears, as he realized the greatness of the girl's sacrifice. He had been advised not to go into Westport. He also knew that his movements were watched. And so the hours slowly passed till the day came for his examination before the Magistrates.

The room was not a small one, but it was packed from end to end by a dense crowd of eager spectators moved by that morbid curiosity which seems to be so characteristic of the uneducated Briton. Victor had found his way to the top of the room, where he sat by his counsel till the time to take his place in the dock, in company with the Professor and Philip Speedwell; the latter restless and anxious, the former cool and collected. The cashier would have spoken with Victor, but he turned away professing not to see the other's proffered hand. Rebecca and Saul Abraham were present; the woman with a merciless glitter in her eyes, and a light of expectation in her deep-lined face; Hazael pale as death, but withal calm and collected.

Presently the Chairman took his seat and the solicitor for the police opened the proceedings with a few remarks bearing upon the case. He alluded to the surprising nature of the crime, and regretted the absence of an important witness, paying at the same time a warm tribute to Miriam's bravery and courage.

For a time the proceedings dragged wearily along. The Inspector of Police in his dry official manner deposed to the fact of being called in, then the Doctor gave his evidence glibly. Victor's advocate rose to cross-examine.

"You have no doubt that deceased died of a wound over the heart, inflicted by some sharp instrument? You are convinced of that?"

The doctor smiled.

"Certainly, and, moreover, death was instantaneous."

"Thank you. Now, deceased was found seated at a table, and must have been struck while seated there; the table is some four feet broad. How do you account for the fact that the blow could have been struck then?"

"My hypothesis is this," returned the Doctor, smiling again. "The blow could not have been struck from in front. It was done from behind."

"With a long, sharp dagger?"

"Precisely. The wound was not very deep—evidently inflicted by a light hand, I have never seen a wound precisely like it before, except a bayonet thrust."

The advocate's face lighted up for a moment. Stooping down amongst his papers, he produced a polished leather case, and drew thereupon a long, keen knife, of peculiar pattern, and embossed handle, which he handed to the witness.

"A knife of that kind, for instance?"

"Precisely. From my recollection, this might be the very weapon."

Counsel said no more. For the present he had gained his point. There was a thrill and a stir in the breathless audience as Rebecca Abraham made her way through the crowd, and stepped into the witness-box. She threw her gaze full upon Victor, who was in the dock now, giving her evidence in a way which told terribly against him. When her tale was finished there was a grim pause for a moment.

"Now," said Counsel for the defence, "I want to ask you a few questions. You showed Mr. Victor Decie up to your son's room?"

"Ay," she answered, slowly. "Ay! and I listened outside the door."

"Ah! a highly credible witness. So you listened outside the door. What did you hear?"

"What did I hear? I heard quarrelling and high words, and oaths; but I did not stay long enough to gather much."

"Your conscience began to get sensitive, presumably. Then, as a matter of fact, you heard nothing—you can remember nothing!"

"Perhaps not," Rebecca mumbled; "but they were quarrelling sorely."

"Pshaw! Some old woman's tale," returned the Advocate, contemptuously. "The Bench will know how to value this evidence at its just worth. You may stand down, woman. You are merely wasting time."

Speedwell climbed reluctantly into the witness-box. There was a well-affected air of veiled regret on his face, a decent hesitation which told in his favour, but he inwardly cowered before the keen eyes of Victor's advocate, for he felt himself on dangerous ground, and his conscience was ill at ease.

Grudgingly he told his tale, little enough in itself, but carefully doled out;

enough to impress the spectators further against Victor Decie. The witness described his wild appearance when he called on the day of the murder, with an apparent hesitation which was more damning than plain, unfaltering evidence. When he had concluded he drew a deep respiration, for the moment he dreaded had arrived.

"You were intimately acquainted with the deceased, I believe?" came the first question.

"Very intimately. We had business transactions together."

"We will come to that presently. Were you aware that deceased held a security on Sir Percival Decie's estate, called The Moat, for twenty thousand pounds?"

"Really," Speedwell faltered, with feigned regret, "I—I scarcely know how to answer this question. In matters pertaining to customers——"

"Do not be afraid, sir," replied the Advocate, with a strange smile; "Sir Percival courts full inquiry. Did you not introduce Sir Percival to the deceased when it was necessary he should have an advance?"

"I certainly did. The deceased came in one day——"

"Never mind one day. Now, upon your oath, was not the whole thing hatched between you and the unfortunate man to get The Moat estate into your power?"

But Speedwell was equal to the occasion. He drew himself up with a glance of haughty surprise and indignation. "It is hardly worth while to deny such an accusation. Really, I cannot submit——"

"Then you, speaking on your oath, do deny it?"

"Most certainly. There is no particle of truth in what you say."

"I am obliged to you, sir. You can stand down."

The spectators breathed again. It was easy to see that some climax had been reached. The chairman wiped his spectacles, and struggled with his handkerchief to conceal a yawn. Apparently, the whole matter was about to collapse for want of further evidence. The police had exhausted their proofs. Then Victor's counsel stood up and announced his intention of calling witnesses. The chairman put up his handkerchief and beamed interestedly through his spectacles upon the speaker, for there was an air of mystery in his manner that indicated something beyond mere professional verbosity.

"Call Mrs. Ruth Meyer," and accordingly she was called; coming forward, wondering apparently what connection she could have with this case. A look of bitter hatred passed between her and Rebecca Abraham, as she took her stand in the witness-box listless and unconcerned.

"You live next door to the house of deceased's parents?"

"Yes, sir; and have the last thirty years."

"Between you, I believe, there is some old standing quarrel?"

"Yes. We have not spoken for nearly five-and-twenty years."

"Very good. And now I understand that the two houses were originally one.

There was once a way of communication between them—an old disused door. How long do you think it was since that was last open?"

"How long!" echoed the witness, pausing. "Years and years."

Counsel took from his pocket a key, and held it up in sight of the whole audience.

"I should like that tried," he said. "Send two of the officers of the court with this key, and try the door. If you cannot open it, my case is at an end."

There was some sensation in court now; they were upon the verge of some great discovery.

The Chairman graciously signified his consent for the experiment to be tried, meanwhile the case could proceed. The advocate proceeded. He handed the long knife to the witness and bade her to examine it carefully.

As she did so a pallid hue crept over her face. The handle was stained here and there with red splashes, the whole blade bore a dull, rusty appearance. Mrs. Ruth Meyer stood with the weapon in her hand, eyeing it as if it had been some noisome reptile.

"Well," sharply came the question, "have you seen that before?"

"Bless you, sir, yes. It is mine; stolen out of the shop this week ago. I—I would swear to it anywhere; but it wasn't stained like this."

The advocate motioned her aside, first retaining the knife, which she fain would have taken in her own custody.

At that moment the policemen returned, both looking preternaturally grave, and laid it on the table. The keen lawyer, versed in the study of faces, gave them a swift, comprehensive glance, and decided to put one of them in the witness-box.

The constable's evidence was brief, but further bore upon the mystery. He had found, he said, that the key not only fitted, but that the door opened on hinges lately oiled, and in the best of order. The excitement was rising again.

But feverish as it had been, it rose still higher as Aurora came forward and took her stand before the tribunal. She was very pale, with a brilliant spot of colour burning on either cheek, and her eyes turned involuntarily in Hazael's direction, who gave her a faint, wan smile of encouragement. At the sight of this fresh, fair face the lawyer's manner toned down to one of suave courtesy.

"You have heard what the last witness has to say?"

"Yes, sir," Aurora answered. "She is my mother."

"Precisely. You listened, I suppose, to the account of your family feud. Now, I want to know if you share in this domestic imbroglio."

Aurora looked puzzled.

"I scarcely understand," she began.

"No? Well, let me put the matter a little more plainly. Mr. Hazael Abraham there is one of the family your mother tells us she has a deadly quarrel with. Now, do you know anything of that young man?"

For a moment the girl hesitated, then, with a courage born of the moment, told the truth.

"I know him intimately," she said. "We are friends."

"Hitherto this has been a profound secret?"

"Yes. Few people have known."

"So you know Abraham well? Well enough to share his troubles."

"Oh, yes! He tells me most things."

"Now, cast your mind back to a morning some time ago, when you met him near Mr. Mark Lockwood's house. To aid your memory, I may say that your sister was accompanying you."

"I remember the morning perfectly."

"Did you notice anything peculiar in his manner?"

"He seemed strangely put out. He stopped me—a thing he does not usually do in the street—and I asked him what was the matter."

"Oh, come!" cried the lawyer earnestly, growing impatient at the long pause. "I beg of you to speak out. Your evidence on this point is most important."

Aurora looked up, and met Hazael's gaze; his white lips moved slightly, and he bent his head in a sign of assent.

"Usually he would not speak to me if my sister was along. Then he was labouring under great excitement. I asked him what was wrong. He told me it was absolutely necessary that he should have a large sum of money immediately. Then my sister spoke."

"Her intellect is not considered strong, I believe?"

"No, sir. So much the contrary that we had either forgotten her or ignored her presence altogether. She startled us by showing that she had listened. She told Haz—Mr. Abraham—where he could get this money. We both laughed, I remember, when she suggested his brother Abishai."

"And you knew this to be out of the question? Now tell me what followed."

"Mr. Abraham left us then, and my sister and I walked home together. Ruth said he must have this money, to which I replied vaguely. Ruth said in her wild manner that if Abishai Abrahams would not find the money she would kill him."

There was a faint titter in the audience. It was the nearest approach to a joke they had yet heard. Victor's advocate hesitated, as if tempted to ask some question, then apparently thrust the temptation away.

"And that is all you have to tell me?

"Yes sir. I can tell you nothing more."

Hazael was the next witness called. He was calm and self-possessed now, for he had steeled his nerves to the encounter, knowing that the secret he had kept so long would soon be food for the idle gossip of Westport. But there was a life at stake, a command which sunk all personal considerations. The defending counsel paused slightly before he asked, "You saw Mr. Victor Decie directly after your brothers death?"

"Yes, sir; immediately afterwards, I should say."

"Did there strike you as being anything strange in his manner."

"He seemed very much disturbed, almost distracted by something."

"Did you have any conversation together?"

"Only a few words. He told me he was going to Rotterdam. I suggested that he would have a rough passage—that was all."

"Very good. Now cast your memory back to the morning upon which you met the last witness and her sister. You mentioned to her that you were in urgent need of a considerable sum of money. Will you be good enough to tell me why you wanted this money?"

Hazael's voice was so low when he replied that his words scarcely reached the anxious, eager crowd. "To replace some securities stolen from my desk."

"Stolen from your desk! Do you mean to tell me that when you missed these securities you informed no one they were gone?"

"No, sir; perhaps I did wrong, but I let the matter remain for a few days, until I was afraid to speak."

"Indeed!" said the lawyer, dryly, as he took a packet of papers in his hand. "Would you be able to identify those bonds again?"

"Yes, sir. I should be prepared to swear to them."

The lawyer passed the papers across, and signified to the witness that he might examine them. Hazael rapidly unfolded the bundle, and regarded them carefully.

Suddenly a smile of relief shot across his face as he handed them back.

"Those are the very bonds!" he said.

The colour which crept into Hazael's face seemed to have been stolen from Speedwell's cheeks. As he turned his fascinated gaze from the papers, he eyes fell upon the Professor, who was regarding him with a mocking smile; his wily cunning could not grasp the situation; he was afraid, and, worst of all, he did not know where the danger lay.

"So those are the securities. We will let that pass for the present. Now you seem, in spite of this Montagu and Capulet feud, to have been on very good terms with the last witness, or you would not have made her your confidant. Is there any attachment between you?"

"There is," said Hazael, firmly, "a very warm attachment."

"Will you be good enough to tell us what that bond of sympathy is?"

Hazael threw back his head, and turned, half-facing the spectators, as he raised his voice to its clearest, most resonant pitch.

"She is my wife!"

A wild murmur of surprise followed his reply. Rebecca and Mrs. Ruth Meyer both half-rose from their seats, glaring at each other. The spectators' heads rose and fell like a troubled sea in the excitement of the moment; even the chairman woke from his doze, and showed a passing interest in the proceedings.

The Professor evinced no palpable surprise, for it was no news to him; the advocate cross-examining smiled behind his white hand, well pleased with the sensation his little dramatic effort had created.

"Now," said he, "we will return to the morning of the murder. You went up with the witness Speedwell and saw the body. After that, did you have any conversation touching the crime with anyone?"

"My sister and I talked it over in the shop."

"Highly probable. Did anything attract your attention, then?"

"Yes, sir. My sister declared she heard footsteps upstairs."

"Did she try to verify her suspicions?

"She certainly went upstairs."

"She went upstairs? Now tell us in a few words what followed."

"She had not been there long before she called me. I went up too. When we got there we found the door between the two houses slightly ajar, and close against the wainscot we picked up a long Indian knife. It was of peculiar pattern, and dripping with blood."

"Was it the knife exhibited now—the weapon claimed by the witness, Ruth Meyer?"

"Yes, sir; it was the same."

Again a shout of surprised astonishment went up from the eager audience. They were feasting on horrors now. A breathless, painful silence fell upon them as the advocate turned to the witness again. He stopped short in his line of examination, and started another thread of his cunning snare.

"You have seen the key which the officer told us fitted the door which leads from your house into Meyer's? Now, have you one like it?"

"I have, sir."

"And I may presume that you have used it in visiting your wife secretly? Now answer me truthfully. Has she a fellow key?"

"She has. I had two made—one for each of us."

"Very well. When you made this discovery, what was done?"

"Nothing. We were too surprised for a time. My sister wanted, in the first place, to see Mr. Decie, who we found had gone to Rotterdam. Against my wish, she determined to cross and see him. Meanwhile I was to say nothing of what we had discovered."

"Since that morning you have had a conversation with a Mr. Denton—Denton, the grocer. Did he tell you he had paid an instalment of some money owing to your late brother on the very morning of his death?"

"He did. And gave me the numbers of the notes."

"Very well. Now on the morning following your sister's departure for Rotterdam you met Ruth Meyer and had a conversation with her. Will you be so good as to tell us what the purport of that interview was?"

"She met me in the street. She appeared more strangely wild than usual. To my surprise, she mentioned the conversation I had with my—my wife the morning the subject of my loss was mentioned. Then she placed in my hand a packet, and immediately left me. I did not intend——"

"Never mind what you intended. Let us say you were taken by storm—astonished. At any rate, the packet remained with you. You opened it?"

"I opened it, and found——"

"Presently. You were present when your late brother's papers were looked through. Did you find any memorandum of the payment of the 500 Mr. Denton alleges to have paid over to your brother?"

"Yes; not only that, but the date and number of the notes."

"Now we shall get at it. We will return to the mysterious parcel. When you opened it, you found something inside?"

"Yes, sir; banknotes."

"And the numbers?"

"Were the same as those which Mr. Denton paid over to my brother on the morning of his murder."

"And the receipt for which Mr. Denton—who I am prepared to put in the box —holds." The lawyer stood up, and threw his pince-nez with a forensic air upon the table. "That is my case, your worships, there is no occasion for me to weary you with a resume of the facts. The rest is in the hands of the police."

There was no sound of violent emotion now, for all eyes were turned upon Ruth Meyer who sat by her mother's side, returning the curious glances with an air of perfect indifference. Was it possible, they thought, that this pale slight girl could have done such a daring thing.

Aurora covered her face and sobbed unrestrainedly on Hazael's shoulder. Her story and its notoriety had been dwarfed into significance now. Presently Ruth Meyer rose with white face and shaking limbs.

"Do you hear?" she gasped—"do you hear? They say you did it—you killed the hunchback to save him! Can't you understand?"

Ruth looked up puzzled for a moment, then the sense of her own notoriety and what she has done seemed to strike her in a pleasant light.

"Killed him!" she cried, nodding and smiling. "Oh, yes. But why make this fuss about it! Poor Hazael! They can't take him to prison now, and Abishai is dead, and I killed him!"

XXI - SPEEDWELL GOES

They found afterwards the unfortunate girl had lost what little reason she had hitherto possessed. She seemed so perfectly indifferent to her crime, so willing to confess the part she had played, that it was impossible to believe that the deed had been done with any realization of its awful consequences. It seemed almost incredible to believe. But now there appeared to be no great probability of ever knowing the real facts of the case. She was removed, perfectly indifferent to her fate, to strong quarters to await her trial. Her family, and Hazael more directly, understood her strange motive, but at present other affairs distracted their attention.

All the next day Trevor Decie and his nephew were closeted with Mark Lockwood and the senior partner in Messrs. Armstrong's bank. The latter had been too prostrated by the sudden failure to attend particularly to business, but now he heard enough to convince him that the disaster had not been brought about by fair, legitimate trading. The quartette sat long in close confabulation, calling the official bank liquidator into their confidence. Unknown to Speedwell, Hazael had been summoned before them touching the loss of his bonds, and his mind was laid at rest by the assurance of his personal indemnity. This meeting had taken place at Lockwood's house. As Hazael was returning homewards he met Aurora on the way.

Her face was set and sorrowful; her eyes red from heavy weeping. It was the first time they had met since yesterday.

"You have told your mother everything?" she asked.

"Yes. But she will listen to nothing yet. We must have patience, and all will be right yet. I have told Mr. Lockwood and his daughter. I found them very kind and sympathetic. Miss Lockwood promised to intercede for me, and she can do anything with my mother. Imagine how they were affected by this fresh proof of Miriam's self-sacrifice!"

"Miriam was a saint," Aurora cried. "And my—our child!"

"You may see her now when you like. I scarcely know what I am talking about; everything is so bewildering and horrible. Aurora, I am acquitted about those bonds. I made a full confession, and they exonerated me completely. I can hold up my head again now."

"And the real thief—who is he?"

"I can guess, but I do not know for certain. Westport has not yet exhausted the list of surprises; but never mind that now. You must be at home this evening early, when Miss Lockwood is going to call on my mother. I shall leave it to her to try and heal the family feud. Let us hope for an end of this bitterness. Heaven knows it has produced misery enough."

"But do you think your mother will listen to Miss Lockwood?" Aurora asked, doubtfully, a vision of that convulsed face and gleaming eyes rising up before her. "Isn't it rather early yet? Oh, shall we ever have any happiness?"

"I hope so," Hazael answered, gravely. "There is trouble and sorrow to spare just now, but already I begin to see sunshine behind. My mother was always fond of me, though she liked Abishai and Miriam better; now I am the only one. My character is cleared. I have Mr. Lockwood's goodwill and promise of assistance; time will do the rest."

Aurora began to see the consolation of these words, for she was young, and youth ever errs upon the side of sanguine hope. Moreover, she had her husband and child free from any concealment now. A little smile trembled on her lips, like a sunbeam peeping from a passing cloud.

"Have you seen Mr. Decie this morning?" she asked.

"That is another friend," Hazael exclaimed, brightening in his turn, "though truly it is a friendship too dearly bought. Yes, I have just seen him. Never fear, Aurora; if our own kith and kin, our own flesh and blood turn against us, we shall never want for friends."

Aurora pointed down the street.

"And he?" she said.

Hazael, looking down, saw Speedwell coming swiftly towards them. His head was cast down, his face was somewhat troubled in the lines about the eyes, and otherwise it was sternly set. He passed on, acknowledging their presence with the semblance of a smile on his thin lips. Hazael clenched his fists involuntarily, as the other passed on, lessening in the distance.

"We have no friend there," he said. "Philip Speedwell never had a friend but himself, and he will want him now, indeed. Let us talk of something else. His name will be on every lip before morning. Come and take a walk with me; it will do you good."

Wholly unconscious of the feelings he had aroused, Speedwell passed on in the direction of Lockwood's residence. Arriving there, he rang the bell with a somewhat exaggerated feeling of importance, and was immediately shown into the library. His self-assured greeting died away upon his lips as he noted the faces of the group seated there; a lump rose up in his throat, and seemed to choke his utterance; he was frightened.

The table was littered with books and papers—ledgers containing long rows of figures and intricate accounts—a puzzle to unpractised eyes, but clear enough to three at least of the company.

"Be seated," Mr. Lockwood commenced, with a stern inflection in his voice— a rare thing for him—"be seated, Philip Speedwell, and give an account of thy stewardship. Friend Yates, thou shalt commence."

No one else had spoken a word. The gentleman called upon—the liquidator— cleared his throat, and commenced to speak in a dry, quiet manner.

"With Mr. Armstrong's assistance, I have been going over the books, and it seems to us that this disaster might have been averted. However, we will not go into that at present. Mr. Speedwell, it is my painful duty to inform you that serious allegations have been made—allegations which impugn your character. You are directly charged with falsifying the books, and appropriating to your own use large sums of money belonging to your late employers. Need I say with what pleasure I shall listen to any statement of yours calculated to dispel this deplorable impression?"

Mr. Yates leant back in his chair, and folded his white hands together, pleased with the succinctness and neatness of his periods. Speedwell glanced round the cold suspicious faces, and as he did so a desperate courage grew up within him, the courage of despair. He was fighting in the dark against an enemy all prepared and ready for the fray.

"I am totally unprepared for this," he said, evenly. "Of course I am ready to meet this serious charge, which, had I been more suspicious, I might have anticipated. Will you be good enough to suspend your indictment."

There was a thin, acid sneer in the words, which brought a faint splash of colour to the first speaker's withered cheeks.

"Very good. In the first place, more than twelve months ago, a sum of 1,000 in Bank of England notes was paid in—to your hands, mind—by the executors of a certain Edgar Lefroy. There can be no mistake, because both the executors were present, and witnessed the transaction. There is no account of this in the books."

"If the money was paid, the ledger will show it," said Speedwell, haughtily.

"Then, for the sake of all parties, I shall be extremely pleased if you will point it out," said the liquidator, drily. "Perhaps you will find the entry."

Speedwell rustled the leaves over swiftly, to hide the tremor of his fingers; but no search of his could disclose the entry, while his face was a picture of strange bewilderment and puzzled mis-comprehension.

"Ah, perhaps I can assist you! The notes were tens—a hundred tens—running from No, 2,458,160 onwards. Do you remember now?"

"No," said the victim, hoarsely. "I do not remember."

Mr. Yates took a letter from his pocket, and smoothed it out upon the table carefully, so that not a crease might remain. He regarded the writing critically, then looked Speedwell in the face with innocent, bland curiosity.

"Mr. Speedwell, who are this firm of Lock and Co., of Greyfriars?"

The miserable man gasped, with his hand to his throat, his face deadly white, a strange palsy shaking him in every limb. Guilt was written on every line of his countenance, damning guilt; and the worst of it was that the silent, grim-visaged group could see it but too well. Yet again he called upon his shaking nerves for one last despairing effort.

"It was their failure which pulled us down, sir. Partly on my own responsibility I did a great deal of bill-discounting business with them—business which ended disastrously. They were a respectable firm———"

"Enough!" Mr. Yates interrupted, sternly. "We are creditors of theirs, I see, for forty thousand pounds. Really, I must congratulate you upon the ingenuity of your scheme. The allegation is that you are virtually Lock and Co."

"It is a lie!" Speedwell exclaimed—"a base, cowardly lie, whoever says so!"

The liquidator passed over the letter he had been so carefully smoothing. As

Speedwell read it, all hope died in his heart. It was the identical note which accompanied the bank notes which the letter-sorter Lord had purloined, and for which he dared not offer a reward. There, in black and white, was the evidence of his guilt, the plot partially disclosed, the promise to send more money at an early date; in fact, a confidential note to a confederate, which effectually disclosed his connection with the bogus Lock and Co.

"It seems against me," Speedwell faltered. "Mr. Lockwood——" But that gentleman turned away with a gesture of contempt. "The man mentioned in this letter deceived me. This George Carroll, whose name is there, could clear my name. But since he has absconded——"

"He has not. The man Carroll was arrested at Brighton last night."

The culprit threw up his hands with a groan of despair. All his neatly-laid schemes had perished at one blow. He waited, with a sickening feeling of anxiety, for his merciless opponent to proceed.

"Lock and Co., we find, are a bogus concern altogether. They certainly have done a large amount of business—on paper; but, with the exception of the funds of Armstrong and Co., they seemed to have touched little or no hard cash. What we wish to know now is where this 40,000 is secreted."

"How should I know?" Speedwell cried. "Do your worst—you can no more."

Mr. Yates bowed in reply, and signified with a wave of his hand that Trevor Decie might proceed.

"I think I can tell you," he commented, "thanks to my gifts of mesmerism. I dare say you have often wondered," he pursued, addressing Speedwell more particularly, "how much you disclosed to me when I had you under the mesmeric influence. You remember probably the agitation you betrayed one night in the Blue Dragon at the sight of a bank note I displayed. I made it my business to trace that note; I also made it my business to bring the letter-sorter, Lord, to book. From him I found out he had purloined the notes, and from him I got the letter Mr. Yates has shown you. I did not say anything then, because I felt by no means certain of my ground; but, having a little business in London, I determined to have an interview with Lock and Co. The manager, Carroll, to my surprise, I found to be an old acquaintance—only his name was not Carroll when I knew him last—and from him, by dint of making use of certain information, I learnt the whole plot. Lock and Co. had failed; but Vanburg Brothers, of Rotterdam, were in a state of thriving prosperity."

The speaker paused to watch the effect of his last words upon Speedwell, who was listening intently. But the bolt had been shot now; no further evidence could make the case blacker, more overwhelming against him. He sat listless and apparently indifferent, hungering to hear now whether his opponents were in a position to trace out the whole of the spoil.

"Vanburg Brothers an Lock and Co. are identically the same," Victor took up the thread. "It was not convenient for the last speaker to leave Westport, so, with the information with which he furnished me, I undertook to go to Rotterdam. I am in a position to assert that Mr. Speedwell is, in fact, Vanburg Brothers, and that the money of Armstrong and Co. is financing that firm. With the assistance of the police I succeeded in seizing their books and papers, also most of their securities, and laid an embargo on their banking account, which is considerable."

"I have Carroll's statement down in writing," Trevor Decie took up the parable again.

"Mr. Decie, you say this money is perfectly safe?"

"Perfectly. I made quite certain of that. And now?"

There was a long pause, broken only by Speedwell's laboured breathing. Everything for which he had bartered his honour was lost now, even the fortune he had hoped to keep in his own hands. Mr. Armstrong arose, his face white and hands trembling, and it was some time ere he recovered his voice.

"Speedwell, you have betrayed a sacred trust in a shameful manner. But I shall not reproach you, though you have well-nigh ruined me. Go," he continued, pointing to the door—"go! So far as I am concerned, you are free. Take yourself away, or I may forget that I am an old man and strike you. Your presence pollutes the very room."

The despised man made a gesture as if he would speak, then, suddenly changing his mind, bowed low, and, turning on his heel, left with one long, lingering look of regret. Perhaps something at the moment jarred upon his hardened heart, some passing emotion like shame.

Mr. Yates sprang to his feet.

"My dear Mr. Armstrong, this is exceedingly irregular," he cried. "I cannot permit——"

"Gently, gently," said the banker, quickly. "I shall not prosecute. I never have done such a thing, and it is too late to begin now. Let him go. So far as I am concerned there is no room for malice in my heart."

Mr. Lockwood smiled approvingly.

"Thou'st right, my friend. Nurse not thy wrath. But I was sadly deceived; yea, sorely. And yet we cannot always judge of faces, as the professor here can tell us."

Trevor Decie answered, his back to them, looking out of the window.

"No; we all make mistakes at times. I was right in my presentiment; but is easy to be wise when you know."

He had succeeded beyond his wildest expectations, yet he experienced a feeling akin to gladness that there should have been found an open door for the criminal. Trevor Decie knew that he himself was not blameless in the matter, and that Speedwell was, after all, his own flesh and blood.

"It is well," Lockwood struck in, folding his hands and bowing his white head, like a priest pronouncing a benediction—"it is well. Time will heal the wounds, and none of you will suffer. For the hand of the Lord hath guided our footsteps, and led us out of danger and tribulation."

They found her next morning, when the tide went down, behind the barrier of the rocks, lying in a tiny pool, with the water laying out her long black hair in shimmering waves. There were no bruises on her fair white skin; no cruel marks to mar the symmetry of her limbs; calm and pale in death as a little child asleep, with a smile upon the scarlet, curved lips such as she had worn in the hour of that noble sacrifice.

Reverent hands raised the dead white form, and bore it sorrowfully homeward. The news had spread, and through the streets, as the still burden passed, folks stood silent, and shutters barred most windows. Home they bore her with gentle step and slow, and Rebecca, seeing them coming, bowed her head and waited, holding Hazael by the hand. Aurora was there, too, for the first time, and longed to speak, but held her peace.

When the bearers had gone they crept upstairs together, and for a few moments contemplated silently the shadowy outline. Then the nature in the woman, touched by a tender flash of memory, arose; she threw herself across the dead girl's breast, refusing to be comforted.

"Mother," said Hazael at length, and his voice trembled, "let me be something to you now, I am all you have left. They are both gone, son and daughter. Let Aurora be another daughter to you."

"For," Aurora faltered, "for I loved her, I loved her, too."

Rebecca kissed the smiling, dead lips; then a strange calm came over her.

She reached out her two hands to the twain, tremblingly.

"It shall be, Hazael, my son, as you have said. For Miriam would have wished it. Oh, if it had not been for this malice and hatred. The God of Israel is against us; he is angry with me! Forgive you! Rather shall you forgive me, my son and my daughter, that the Lord has vouchsafed to me to my declining years?"

XXII - THE PROMPTER'S BELL

As the wheel of life goes round it brings changes and alterations, care and sorrow, joy and happiness alternatively, to us all. Gradually the strange incidents and startling events were forgotten as the months went on, and summer came round again, bringing the dog-roses and the warmth of leafy June, a fitting time of gladness and sunshine to group our characters together, and all happiness, and peace, and joy everlasting.

Saul Abrahams had taken his crimes and misfortunes, his bitter memory to the grave, where all things are forgotten. After Abishai's death he had pined away and died. At the last he wandered, calling for his old master, and they wondered that he should derive such comfort from the presence of the Professor, who was with him at the last alone, when that troubled spirit had stilled for ever. The Professor said, with unaccustomed brevity, that it was strange, then turned the subject, for he was touched by this proof of inalienable sincerity.

In the sporting papers there appears from time to time an advertisement of a racing firm at Boulogne-Sur-Mer; a glowing announcement of the great fortune to be made by any bold speculator who has command of capital to the extent of half a crown. From the regularity with which the announcement appears, we have every reason to believe that the speculation is a flourishing one. The head of the firm, so rumour says, bears a strong likeness to Philip Speedwell; and, indeed, the Professor, on one of his flying visits to the favourite resort for the Briton "who has done something wrong," to quote a once popular poem, admitted to have seen Speedwell apparently enjoying a state of undeserved prosperity. But even upon this point he is wont to observe an unusual reticence. After a time the shutters which had for so long barred the windows of Messrs. Armstrong's bank were taken down again. People gave knowing nods and shrugged their shoulders; but gradually it became known that most of the purloined capital had been recovered, and flagging faith was greatly restored. But when it was seen that Mark Lockwood had again opened an account with them, popular opinion turned in their favour, and Messrs. Armstrong soon became stronger than ever, a result which was augmented in a great measure by the popularity and business qualities of the new manager, who, of course—it is idle to deceive you—was none else than Hazael.

There was at first some demur to his appointment but, as Mr. Lockwood—who had stood by his friend throughout—pointed out, they owed him something, and, the merchant's request being almost a command, the appointment was made. And, as usual, Mr. Lockwood was right, Hazael proving to be the right man in the right place. So he went to live at the bank with his wife and the baby, which latter they had to obtain by stratagem from Miss Lockwood, who had conceived for it an affection which seriously threatened, so said Victor Decie, to interfere with his matrimonial views. The old pawnbroker's shop had been abandoned, and Rebecca lived with the young couple. It was an excellent arrangement; for, since Abishai's death, she had found herself the mistress of a handsome fortune, which meant many luxuries to the young couple which the salary of the newly-started bank could scarcely be expected to afford.

Ruth's crime had been treated with pitying care. She had been put upon her trial; but she was so perfectly insane that she was ordered to be detained during Her Majesty's pleasure. After a time strong influence was brought to bear, and she was removed from the criminal lunatic asylum to more careful hands, where she is supremely happy in her blissful ignorance and kindly treated, though a constant watch is set upon her movements. But, up to the present, there has been no disposition to break out observed. Her name is seldom mentioned, and then under the breath in accents of purest pity.

Gradually as time went on, Sir Percival Decie, who erstwhile had merely asked to be taken out and buried with his outraged ancestors, showed a disposition to revive, and by degrees reached the stage when he alluded to himself as the victim of diabolical machinations. From thence his recovery was rapid. He began to hold up his head again, and resumed his attendance at the Magistrates' meetings.

By the assistance of Mark Lockwood he succeeded in ridding himself of his most pressing liabilities, and the Old Meadow copper seam was opened. It proved to be a gigantic success, and in a short time he was not only free from all pecuniary embarrassments, but upon the highroad to die a millionaire. But he steadily refused to soil his fingers with any more commercial enterprise, leaving the management of affairs to Victor, who, under Lockwood's guidance, had developed considerable business ability.

By way of showing gratitude for this truly disinterested kindness, and the above-mentioned infant being restored to his anxious parents, Victor commenced a nefarious scheme to get Ida from her parental roof, and make her his wife. So persistent was he in this undertaking, aided and abetted by Sir Percival, that Miss Lockwood, being of an amiable and yielding disposition, gave a reluctant consent, with Mark Lockwood acquiescing to the inevitable. So, one fine May morning, not quite a year later, they were married quietly, to the disgust of the people of Westport, who turned out in large numbers, and pelted the happy couple with rice and flowers, with that hearty goodwill characteristic of the 'north countrie.' There were many deputations and congratulatory addresses—one from the working men of Westport, presented by a notorious poacher.

"What next?" Sir Percival growled, though he was pleased enough. "Victor, you must be a Radical! They never cared so much for me. Bah! the country is going——"

"To perdition, sir, of course," Victor laughed. "Let the men alone, you misanthrope! Can't you see how it flatters my youthful vanity?"

"Well, it's a sign of goodwill, anyway," said the Baronet, mollified. "You're a good lad, Victor, and you have a pleasant, sympathetic manner, a thing I never had. And now, for the sake of your old dad, don't be long away. I am not so young as I used to be, and the last twelve months has aged me a little. So remember that you are leaving behind two lonely old men, and——"

Victor grasped his father's hand fervently, saying nothing. But I think they understood. Then they stepped into the carriage which was to take them some miles on their way to the lakes. But the populace were too many for them; already they had the horses out, and were charging down the drive into the road. And foremost in the fray were the poachers, dragging them with hearty good-will, cheered on by the Professor, who had thrown his hat and gloves to the wind, and presented the spectacle of a well-dressed elderly gentleman who had been drawn through a hedge backwards.

"But," said Sir Percival, a little petulantly, "Trevor has no sense of what was befitting to the family dignity."

The crowd dragged the happy pair out into the highroad between the hedges all fragrant with the pink-flushed dog-roses; dragged them till Victor half-peremptorily commanded them to stop. The notorious poacher signified to his crowd to obey, and held his hand over the carriage-door, and Ida, nothing abashed, shook it warmly. In boastful vain-glorious moments the man still tells the tale.

There was another reason why they wished to be alone. They passed through Westport to the other side, into the fair, sweet country again. Here, for a moment, they stopped, for it was the cemetery. Just through the iron gates was a simple white cross, and on this Ida lay a wreath of flowers she had brought for the purpose. For some time they stood looking down in silence.

"It was a noble, noble sacrifice, Victor."

"'Tis, my darling; so great, that I can hardly realize it now. But regrets are vain and fleeting. She is happy now, poor, troubled spirit. Come, let us get away now. I do not care to see a shadow on your face to-day."

So they drove away through the smiling, open country, and the white stone covering that gallant heart was forgotten for a time. But in the even time, when the light is dim and low, their hearts turn to Miriam with a glow of tender recollection.

THE END